THE COLLECTOR DECEPTION

Book Seven: Masquerade Inc.
Cozy Mysteries

PATTI LARSEN

Thanks, Kirstin!

ISBN-13: 978-1-989925-39-3

MOMENT DE LA MORT

*H*E LOVES HER, HAS *loved her since he bought her for a fraction of what she's worth. Best purchase ever.*

Except it's time to say goodbye, because the money? Just too good to turn down.

He sighs, adores her for one last moment, even as hands close on the lanyard around his neck and pull tight. No time to struggle or fight. No strength to save himself.

She does nothing to help, a quiet observer, as he dies in her arms.

He's hardly her first loss, so what did he expect?

CHAPTER ONE

WHO WAS IT WHO thought this was a good idea, flying all the way to California to check out a car I never liked (okay, hated to the depths of my soul with a passion that only a little girl scorned by her own mother could feel), sent to do so thanks to an assassin I couldn't trust while running away from the fact I was fighting with my adopted family over this exact issue and from the truth I was still in love with my ex-husband while adoring the woman he was now dating?

Oh. Right. It was *my* bright idea. I'm an idiot.

The fact my best friend and rock star, got your back, most amazing woman ever, Reggie Nolan, agreed to come with me was one of the only reasons I followed through on this uber ridiculous decision to put myself into a position to trigger old hurts and hates and maybe find some closure on the murder of my mother if that was even a real thing and not some construct of psychotherapy that never worked for me anyway.

Oh, the run-on sentences bothering you in my stream of consciousness attempt to escape from the reality of my present situation? Too bad. I was having a hard enough time corralling my spinning mind as I stood in the nasty air conditioning of the Hollywood Haven Hotel, lacking sleep since I'd spent maybe an hour in my bed in our suite upstairs trying to convince my brain to stop spinning. Even a hard-core treadmill run in the overly-bright hotel gym at midnight hadn't tired me out sufficiently to get any amount of rest.

Wound up? Just a little. Wishing I was out in the bright sunshine or back in Martingale in my apartment with my ginger tabby purring and kneading my chest. Anything to escape this scenario I'd put myself in. Which meant I stayed put because it was the wrong choice, epic Petal Morgan. Anyone else would have let themselves off the hook and chosen happiness over beating this particular dead actress (okay, that was an awful analogy, even for me). Anyone else with the sense the Universe gave them.

Not me, apparently. So there I stood, suffering in silence, with a freaking lanyard around my neck, the plastic covered badge dangling from it identifying me as one Kelly Grace. Reggie's giggling nod to, you guessed it, the famous actress didn't raise the smile she'd hoped for, while she got to be Berry Hale because my best friend had a terrible sense of humor.

No, I was the one without mirth or any kind of happiness. And whose fault was that? Looking at you, missy.

Not that it mattered anyway. This wasn't an op, a job, a deception. Nothing I could call normal in my abnormal existence of faking my way through jobs that paid me the big bucks. No one was going to pad my bank account for uncovering truths and lies or finding out why someone died (I already knew why Mom died, right?). So why then was I putting myself through this horrible experience when the payoff seemed not only dismal but distant and, more than likely, nigh onto impossible?

I'd had a lot of years to get over Mom's murder.

Hadn't happened yet.

This was my life I was purposely messing with, so why I agreed to the falsehood of healing opportunities and grief stages and finding my truths (gag me, please, no spoon required you 80s kids) all came down to one simple truth. While Annette Morgan was long dead (poor little Petal lost her mommy, what a shame and a bother), a recent resurgence in interest in my mother's career surfaced thanks to some advertising genius (jackass) who decided the farewell scene of her last movie—*Lucille*, no less, the name of the very car I was here to say adieu to—in a current ad campaign had people remembering her name, her beauty and all the good stuff.

Thing was, the good stuff was a sham. Pull the

wool over your eyes, don't check behind the curtain or believe a thing you read on the internet. All of it one big, giant whitewashed fraud.

Nope, no go on the good here. But the bad? Oh, it was *endless*.

I ducked my head in line when the guy ahead of me glanced back, frowning. I'd failed to bring a wig or change my appearance, brilliant for a deception expert, though you'd have to forgive me since I wasn't in my right mind at the moment. Instead, I shoved the giant mirror sunglasses I'd brought with me further up my nose and turned my head, hoping it was sufficient, the lights overhead catching the lenses and throwing glare his way.

I would have preferred to throw shade, but this was the best I could do with what I had right now.

"Should be any second." Reggie hooked her arm through mine, actually excited and I let her be, didn't want to harsh the buzz she'd been bouncing around in since I asked her to come with me two days ago, since we boarded the plane yesterday afternoon, for the drive to the hotel in the limo she'd sprung for. I just smiled and pretended everything was hunky dory, that I hadn't had a massive argument with said adopted fam just twenty-fourish hours ago.

Oh, not the whole fam, no. And not the expected fam, either. In fact, the one person I'd fully thought would be on my side lost his freaking mind when I corralled Dad, Pops and Jordan in the living room of the main house to tell them why I was on my way to the airport.

"You can't just leave well enough alone?" Jordan's instant rejection of the idea had me floored, let me tell you. My baby brother's fury had to come from somewhere, but I had no idea the source. He had leaped to his feet, shaking a fist at me (the dude was a yoga instructor. I pissed off a yogi, guys, that's how awesome I am) and yelled all kinds of things about family and betrayal and real fathers and dumb things I just let him say and rant about. While I fought off tears and the little brother I adored, with his gorgeous dark face contorted in fury and despair, stormed out and past me and slammed the front door like he was never coming back.

Like he hoped I never would.

Whatever was up with my brother, my fathers had sat back to give him space, like they always did with both of us. It was Pops, naturally, who took the first step toward making me feel better when that was, frankly, an impossibility, my adorable Asian father in his beige cardigan with the leather elbow patches (such a nerd, I loved him for it) tried to be all supportive-like while Dad—my looming, stoic FBI sparkly oh-so-specially Caucasian shiny suspicious agent Dad with his grim expression and his inability to bend—let his ethics professor husband try.

And try. Poor Pops.

I can't remember what else I said, though when Dad did ask a question, it was the one I dreaded the most.

"Where did this information come from, Petal?" Because you had to believe my law enforcement sniffer dog hound of a knew me better than anyone father honed in on exactly where the weak and wobbly nature of this entire plan fell apart.

I could have lied, told him I dug it up myself, showed them both the photo. While choosing the truth road to father fear hell, explaining who the Chameleon was, that nemesis assassin player of deception who reminded me too much of me at times though she was the bad guy (right?).

Pops stared at me like I'd lost my mind. While Dad...

Sighed. And left the room.

I fumbled the ball. Tried to explain to Pops, my only cheerleader left, this wasn't about Lucille, not really. Nor about finding my "real" father. This was about Mom and me and letting her go before my clinging to the past and who she'd made me—who I'd become thanks to my first eight years in her screwed-up presence—could wreck my life further and how not dealing interfered with who I knew I could be.

If I could only let her go.

Pops did his best to comfort me, waved when I drove off to pick up Reggie. But even he, I knew, ached so deeply for this choice I'd made I likely did more damage to the people who loved me most in the world than I'd ever done before. Or they deserved.

They deserved a daughter who loved them unconditionally, who wasn't a screw-up who could only find work lying about who she was and, guess what, wasn't just good at it but great. Like, should lie all the time if it works out this well great. What did that say about me exactly? Not a lot. And Jordan? He deserved a sister who could listen to his problems without dumping her own on him, who gave him support instead of angst.

Rafe.

Oh, not going there.

Not.

My mind flickered back to that promise to Pops. Not wanting or needing my biological dad in my life. I had two already that I loved with every fiber of me that was able to love despite what my mother's influence created. And who drove me nuts at the same time. I did *not* need a third.

I didn't. Did I? This wasn't about him. It was about Mom.

Remember the part about being a good liar? Yeah, I was a genius because I practiced on myself.

And then Reggie tugged on me and I was here, present and accounted for, the line finally moving through the hotel, out of the lobby and through to the event location, the very hotel we were staying at, in fact, because I'd planned that well.

Because I wanted to be close to Lucille.

"Are you ready?" Reggie met my eyes with her own black ones unblinking, that gorgeous face of hers intent, worried now as my anxiety and screwed up brain finally registered.

Until I faked a smile, shrugged. "No," I said. "But let's do it anyway."

CHAPTER TWO

T HE AUCTION SPACE HAD been set up by category, our badges letting us through to the main room lined with glass display cases, a variety of merchandise up for bid in shiny relief under bright lights.

I barely saw any of the smaller pieces, Reggie pausing now and then to peek inside a case, muttering this and that to me as she recognized something from a famous TV show or movie, or a piece owned by a star past their prime.

My eyes were locked on the red velvet curtain at the back of the room, the circular shield hanging from a round pipe on the ceiling, waiting for the big reveal. Lucille was the star of the show, after all, the present owner excited, according to the digital pamphlet I'd looked over on the plane, by the resurgence of all things Annette Morgan, looking for a new home for the prized possession of that most tragic of lost stars.

Gag.

Reggie finally dragged my attention away from the impending doom that seemed to loom over the reveal, prodding me to stay with her. I fought to, wanted to, if only so she didn't look at me with that growing anxiety on her face.

"Do I have to worry about you, girlfriend?" She made me face her, hands grasping mine, shaking me just a little. "Petal Morgan, do I need to smack you or something?"

I laughed at that, hugging her abruptly. "I wouldn't want anyone else to be here with me right now," I said. "Keep me grounded, okay?"

She nodded against my cheek, her full corkscrew curls shining as she pulled away, about as much as the rim of tears in her eyes. She tugged me toward a glass case, pointing out the description. "Can you imagine buying someone's toilet?" She wrinkled her nose, another giggle escaping me. "I don't care if it is accented in gold." She led me onward, making funny, snide and typically Reggie comments about everything we encountered, my best friend doing her best to keep me with her.

And succeeded.

I felt like I could breathe when she distracted me, that I wasn't about to come face-to-face with my past in the worst possible venue, had to remind myself it was just a stupid car. Just a stupid freaking red '62 Corvette convertible with the characteristic white stripe down the side and stunning whitewall tires, the red leather interior and powerful engine, the very car my mother took me for a single ride in, once and once only, after bringing her home from set.

Flinch. I wasn't ready for that memory yet.

Might never be.

Instead, I focused on Reggie, chose her, chose the chattering around me, international buyers with their accents and foreign languages circling each item, buyers on phones talking with other buyers, the detritus of fame and lost fortune gathered together in this place, put on display to be bought and sold while the real history was lost forever.

Okay, come back, Petal.

Breathe.

That's it. Just breathe.

How had we moved so quickly around the left side of the room, now finally in the place I dreaded and craved and longed for and already hated with a passion that had sweat breaking out on my upper lip? I wiped it clear, doing my best to hide the growing stress from Reggie, accepting all the love and distraction she could offer but coming to a purposeful halt just outside the red velvet rope that hid the platform behind that red velvet curtain to the red car on the other side.

Why was everything red?

Someone bumped me, pulling me back from my death glare at the wall of fabric hiding Lucille from me. I looked up in irritation, my sunglasses no help in here, tucked into the neckline of my t-shirt and my face, now fully exposed, turned up in sullen agitation.

He stared at me, eyes widening, the tall dude in the Lucille T-shirt—yeah, they made those—who glanced down at the name on my badge before taking me in again, his lower lip trembling, his girth, not exactly fat but not muscular either, vibrating as he towered over me and stared.

I knew he knew. Stared right back, not knowing where this challenging defiance came from and not caring, liking the feel of it, the power in standing my ground. Yeah, dude, that's right. Petal Morgan. Annette's daughter. Get a good freaking look, because that's all you're getting.

Reggie slipped in between us, breaking the rapport. "Let's get a drink," she murmured, her sharp nails digging into the flesh of my wrist. "I'm thirsty, are you thirsty?"

The big guy moved off without saying a word. Which broke the spell and had me trembling and sweating all over again.

"Yeah," I said. "A drink. Great idea." Probably the worst possible idea, actually, because drinking in this state? Who knew what I'd do?

I didn't. And that was a scary truth I'd have to live with. Hopefully without finding out.

Before we could turn and go to the bar at the far end of the room—the furthest from Lucille and likely Reggie's next distraction strategy—a man in a navy suit with a flashy red tie and pocket square (it had to be red, didn't it?) stepped up onto the edge of the platform with a beaming smile on his perfect

California tanned face with his shiny white veneers flashing in the spotlight that spun and settled on him.

"Ladies and gentlemen!" He had that polished voice of a man who'd spent far too many years in Hollywood, or maybe on a stage in Vegas. Plastic as the rest of him. Okay, I was grumpy and not in a charitable mood, but I know you know the kind of guy I mean. Game show chic. "Welcome to our auction. I'm Paxton Hunter, your host, and tonight, we bring you the finest memorabilia the entertainment industry has to offer!" There was enough applause he carried on like he'd been awarded a standing ovation. "I'm sure you're all as excited as I am to lay your eyes on the main event." More applause, some cheers. Mom would have loved it. He gestured to the curtain behind him, still beaming that fake smile. "Behind this red velvet is the car of your dreams." He swept his arm forward, taking us all in, though if he thought it was the car of my dreams he had another thing coming. Okay, my nightmares, if that counted. "But, before we get to the main event, I'd like to draw your attention to some of the finest pieces on the market today."

Great. We were going to have to stand here and watch the girls in the slinky ballgowns parade past him with each and every freaking item talked about ad nauseam even though they were all laid out in the brochure?

I'd barely been here a half hour and I'd already had enough. "I'll get us those drinks." I abandoned Reggie to the unfolding show, needing to be alone, knowing if she came with me I'd be short with her and she didn't deserve that. I just needed a second, to breathe, to get a drink in me and maybe two and take a firm grasp on the memories surfacing and fighting for attention

—*hiding in her closet, hearing her scream, curled into her clothes and the smell of her as he beat her to death*—

Grunt.

I made it to the bar without punching anyone, so there was that little victory to cling to. I even managed to order four drinks—you better believe I was double fisting—and paid for the plastic cups filled with wine (for Reggie) and gin and tonic (for me), carrying them like a pro to the corner of the bar while I knocked back my first one in four long swallows and took the first step toward finding out what I would actually do if drunk and this situation came together.

Hey, it was a hike back to Reggie and I couldn't carry four that far.

Uh-huh. Believe that? Got a bridge to sell you.

"I assumed you'd be here." Someone spoke so near me I jumped a little, turned to find the handsome and suited man speaking, not to me, but a slim and dour young woman in a skin-tight black suit, her Asian features more Japanese than Chinese. I only knew because Pops insisted, his frustration in American inability to differentiate between nationalities one of his pet peeves.

"Yosef," she said. "You know he wants Lucille. At any price."

"We'll see, Ashe," the Middle Eastern man, his accent placing him as possibly Israeli, smiled at her, diamond ring flashing on his right index finger. "He doesn't always get everything he wants."

She inclined her head. Glanced my way, eyebrow raising.

Time to go.

When I turned to do just that, I almost ran into a middle-aged blonde, her cell phone clamped to her ear, expression angry enough I jerked back, trying to maneuver around her while others closed the gap and left me trapped a moment.

"And I'm telling *you*," she snarled into the phone, "he's not *here*." Pause. "It's not like Edison to miss a chance at being the center of attention." Another short pause while I gestured at a tall young man to move only to be ignored. Awesome. "My husband wouldn't let the auction happen without him. He's been wanting to sell that stupid car for months." That caught my breath and my attention and instead of trying to escape, I froze, stared at the woman who finally looked up and took note of me, of her body position in my way.

And moved.

While I held still another second.

"Just tell me if he calls," she said, now sounding a little worried. "I don't want to have to be the one to stand on that stage and hand over the keys to the new owner." She hung up and moved on while my heart pounded.

It shouldn't have gotten to me, not really. So

what I'd been standing next to the wife of the guy who owned Lucille? Talk about degrees of uninspired and unimportant separation. But, for whatever reason only known to my PTSD, being in proximity with someone who had spent time with my mother's car felt like a betrayal.

Get a freaking grip already.

I did manage to wrangle four glasses back to Reggie (if you're counting that means I had three already because I turned back to the bar and ordered another after that little encounter and wasn't planning to stop anytime soon) without spilling any or, again, punching anyone (because that would mean spilling and, no, just no). She accepted her two glasses without comment, sipping the first, while I tucked in next to her, finishing my second drink and stacking the glass beneath the third as dudebro jerkface finally got to the freaking point already.

"Thank you, ladies, weren't they lovely?" Yeah, whatever, the smattering of applause felt as fraudulent as his smile. "I'm done keeping you waiting."

My phone buzzed. Crap timing, but I slipped it from my back pocket and checked it anyway.

I hope you find what you're looking for.

I almost fired off a nasty response but didn't. Whatever the Chameleon's motivation for this, she had what she wanted. I was in California again for the first time since I was a lost and lonely child. About to face down the focus of all the rage and vitriol that was left of my feelings for my mother.

Instead of giving her satisfaction, I put the phone away, feeling the warmth of too much alcohol drunk far too quickly hit my system as Paxton Hunter finally wrapped things up. "This afternoon, we have the pleasure, the honor, the absolute privilege of presenting a true icon of Hollywood. My friends, please put your hands together for," he paused for dramatic effect and I wanted to punch him in the face, "Lucille!"

Someone pulled the cord beside the curtain, one of the girls, I guess, I wasn't paying attention. As it slid open and the spotlight over my mother's pride and joy fired to life in a halo of revealing light, I caught my breath.

Stared.

And started to laugh. A deep, pained laugh that tore at my chest and throat and hurt so very much I couldn't bring myself to stop. Not because of Lucille, she was bad enough, oh no.

Because the man in the photo the Chameleon sent me sat in the front seat, just like the picture. Except instead of a happy grin? He smiled a rictus of death.

CHAPTER THREE

WELL, HOW FAMILIAR WAS *this* scene? Though, I had to admit, tipsy or not, I missed the sight of Detective Elle Gordon and even the puss-faced disapproval of her nasty partner, Rick Danone, instead standing back with Reggie while LAPD detectives chatted with a pair of FBI agents.

Oh yeah, they'd pulled out the big guns, my history with Dad whispering to Reggie why the feds were there. "All this stuff," I said, waving my drink that really could have been stronger because I should be drunk by now after the effort I made, "comes from international buyers. And the owner of that," I jabbed a finger at Lucille, "is from out of state. Which means, ta-da! Sparkle Agents Extraordinaire." I took another sip. "You're welcome."

Reggie half-scowled, half-laughed. "You take it

easy on that," she said, pointing at my gin and tonic. "The last thing we need is to draw attention, right?"

Right. Of course. Though as I observed the two agents, the woman turned and noticed me, her eyes widening, her long stride carrying her to us like magic. Because that was my luck, wasn't it? Oh yes siree, Bob's your uncle.

"Petal Morgan." She held out her hand, shaking mine when I wiped off the condensation from my drink and shook back, the cool dryness of her touch firm. She glanced at Reggie but didn't ask her name, introducing herself to me. "You wouldn't remember me. I know your father." She cleared her throat. "Special Agent Celia Dune."

"Nice to meet you," I said. "Wait, remember you?"

She nodded then, hand dropping to her side, flicker of something I couldn't read crossing her face. "I was there. That night." She coughed softly again, uncomfortable now. "When you lost your mother."

Ah.

Fabulous.

"Regina Nolan." My bestie had clearly taken offense to being brushed off and I hardly blamed her.

"Reggie, this is Agent Dune," I said with the barest hint of sarcasm, like she hadn't been standing there the whole time, the pointed way I introduced her the only apology for the woman's rudeness I could offer at the moment. Not exactly the chastising barb I could have mustered under other circumstances, but it would have to do. "She knows Dad."

My best friend's dark eyes acknowledged my attempt, barest smile lifting her full lips as she sighed softly, arm around my shoulder, meeting the agent's eyes when she frowned.

"It's been rough," she said, no softness in her voice at all. "Petal's a little… overwhelmed."

Agent Dune's expression instantly shifted back to that weird flicker of whatever it was haunted her while I wondered how she managed her bob and weave from emotion to emotion. Could normal people do that? Just change how they felt so fast?

Cool.

Yes, it was very apparent to me I was, in fact, on my way to drunk and while it would have been a lovely trip to the rest of the way to inebriated, I purposely turned and set the remains of my drink on the ledge of one of the display cases before giving Agent Dune my full attention.

After all, I had a front seat to whatever continuing de-evolution the Universe had planned and being blackout drunk defeated the purpose. I needed to be conscious to fully appreciate how badly this went when I pondered it at length later.

"You were saying." I waited for her to go on, both hands crammed into the back pockets of my jeans.

"Nothing, I'm sorry." She hesitated, then shrugged. "How's Andy?"

I fought off a sarcastic reply. "Dad's great," I

said. "Not so happy I'm here, but great otherwise."

She accepted that with a knowing nod, like she knew anything about me or why I came to California and had the right to pretend she did—

—the woman stood in the crack of the closet doorway, her face a stern mask—

"I remember you," I blurted. Weird how that surfaced suddenly. I'd had a set collection of memories I'd gnawed at and finally buried as best I could since the night Mom died. I guess being confronted with someone who'd been there, someone I'd met or seen, triggered the moment.

The question was, however, why did my admitting so make Agent Dune flinch when she was the one who brought it up in the first place? Did something happen I still couldn't recall and was it worse than I remembered? Something to do with Dad or—

Petal.

Breathing, remember? We were breathing.

I caught sight of big and lumbering lingering nearby and groaned, knowing I was outed now for sure, a few people turning to look, to notice who the sparkly agent talked to, that my face and her face— my mother's face—were nearly identical and if I wanted anonymity on this little trip?

Yeah, this wasn't the road to that.

Agent Dune seemed to realize she'd pointed a laser target right at me because she shifted in discomfort, glancing around. "I'm sorry," she said. "Did you see anything that might help?"

"Not a blessed thing," I said, happy that was true, for once. "One second we were here, waiting for the car's grand reveal and the next, whoopsie. Dead guy in the front seat. Though I do know that's the owner." Paused, thought about it. Wait, was he my real dad? "He is, right? The owner?"

Dune nodded, frowned. "Yes, Edison Fisher," she said. "Did you know him?"

"Nope," I said. "Well, he's the reason I'm here, but I never met him." Good thing you stopped drinking, Petal. Jeeze, get a grip.

"What Petal means," Reggie said, cutting in before I could carry on and further embarrass myself, "is that she received information and a photo that the dead man was selling her mother's car. So we came to say goodbye to Lucille, right, Petal?" She smiled sadly at me with a flash of warning in her dark eyes and those incredibly sharp nails now prodding my ribs before she returned her sorrowful expression back to the agent. "Closure. You understand."

Agent Dune seemed to, another grave nod following Reggie's hasty explanation. Thing was, it was the truth. I almost laughed at that because usually at this point I was in the middle of lying through my teeth, not actually handing over honesty.

Maybe this was a good idea after all.

"Thank you for your candor," Agent Dune said, one hand rising to touch my arm, dropping away before making contact. "I still relive that scene sometimes, Petal. Finding you." She swallowed, looked away. Yay, thanks for the reminder, agenty agentpants. Like I didn't relive it myself, only I was a little girl, you heartless—

Inhale.

Exhale.

"It's nice to see you're doing well," she said then and I snorted. Giggle snorted, actually, Reggie jerking on me hard enough I looked up and met her eyes.

"Well, it's funny, right?" I couldn't help the bubbling wave of hysterical laughter that came out of me, despite the stares and the obvious lack of decorum such amusement in the middle of a suspicious death in the front seat of my mother's old car might have normally warranted. I'd blame the gin, but I knew better.

I was cracking the feck up and there was nothing to do but let it happen and hope Reggie had the heart to pick up the pieces.

"I lie to people for a living," I told the agent, her eyes widening slightly, frown returning. "Yup, I'm a deception expert. Solve murder cases, even." I gestured at the scene behind the now closed curtain again, where I knew forensics folks in their ugly coveralls were doing their due diligence. "I'm pretty good at it. So yeah. I'm awesome."

"I imagine Andy disapproves of that." Her lips quirked. Maybe it should have endeared me to her, but the way she judged my father for protecting me? She didn't get to do that. I was the only one who was allowed to criticize him for giving me a hard time.

It was what it was. I didn't say it had to make sense. Sheesh.

"I come by it honestly." I shrugged, defending Dad and Mom and my messed-up life in the face of this stranger who thought she knew me, who I'd met, like, once on my worst night ever. "Lying's in my blood, I guess. Look at how good Mom was at it." Why did that make me sad all of a sudden? Because I just compared myself to my mother and that was the most tragic connection I could ever make, drunk or sober.

Agent Dune's weird expression was back, but I was too tipsy to figure it out and decided I didn't care anyway. Hopefully this was the last time I'd be seeing her so she could keep her personal feelings to herself.

"I wish you the best, Petal." She grasped my hand, let me go quickly, almost like touching me burned her. "And while I'm sure your talents lend to being a great investigator, I'll ask you to steer clear of my crime scene."

I saluted her as she walked away, Agent Dune nodding to Reggie in farewell.

While my best friend hissed in my ear. "Are you out of your mind?"

I met her eyes. Grinned. Winked. "That's the question, isn't it? I think the answer might be yes."

She didn't appreciate my giggle fit or the response but there was nothing I could do about either one.

CHAPTER FOUR

I WOULD HAVE LOVED to have left then and there, but they made us wait as everyone was questioned, not a soul allowed to leave until we'd all at least had a few minutes with the LAPD detectives or those special agents in charge.

At least as the hour or so passed I sobered up somewhat, the weak pour the bartender made, while irritating from a financial standpoint, at least meaning I wasn't a drunken mess for long. Lack of sleep and food had a hand in my condition, I had no doubt, though the contributing factors to my tipsiness also meant the faux drunk I'd experienced disappeared without further imbibing. Not that I was dead cold sober by the time to cops wrapped up or anything, but I was no longer that out of control spiraling mess who had Reggie's nails digging into her ribs every five seconds.

I sighed as we sat against the section of wall she'd chosen for our huddle, me leaning into her, awareness returned sufficiently sorrow and guilt set in again. My go-to favorite.

"What a disappointing end to a truly epic and awful idea." I shot her a sad smile, forcing myself to sit up and not be such a physical burden, at least, even if there wasn't much I could do about the emotional. "I'm so sorry I dragged you out here, Reg. This is not how I was hoping it would go." Especially since she'd barely had time to catch her breath after the last job we did together. Thinking her babysitting another drunk while almost getting shot had me wincing. "These little adventures with me are going to give you an ulcer."

She bumped shoulders with me, her wine long discarded, dark eyes fixed on me. "I chose to come," she said. "And despite what you might think, I'm happy to be here." Reggie turned her head, looking out over the crowd, most of whom had chosen to do what we did and sit, giving us a clear line of sight to the curtains and Lucille's podium. "Look, I have no idea what you were expecting, but yeah. I get that you're disappointed. But it's not your fault, Petal, so you don't have to apologize. I know what it's like to want to resolve your past." She had her own family issues, not the least of which was her crime family father, though we'd never talked about it and now I felt guilty about that, too. "If it helps or not, you would have regretted not trying." She twisted around, frowning. "I'm going to find a washroom. You want to come?"

I shook my head. "I'm good. I'll keep your seat."

She hugged me quickly before standing, staring down at me. "It's going to be okay, Petal." And left before I could respond.

If she said so. Trouble was, I'd been told that before. By a tall and handsome young FBI agent who found me after my mother was killed. I'd believed him and trusted him and gone with him, clung to his assurances that everything would, in fact, be okay.

How had he been so wrong?

The main issue with Reggie leaving? I no longer had a bodyguard, and yes, she had training in that department, though I was sure she hadn't expected to have to play that role again so soon. Considering I'd made about as big a fool of myself as the last person she'd been hired to guard (okay, I wasn't that bad) she had to be regretting her life choices right about now.

I know I was. And didn't know how to stop the inevitable as the big guy who'd bumped me, his Lucille T-shirt making me wince, approached on tentative feet, lurking and lingering a long time, nervous glances my way making me angry.

"What?" I knew it wasn't his fault and snapping at him like that wasn't helping but I was getting a headache from coming down off the gin and the murder and Lucille and my memories and I frankly wasn't in the mood to coddle some fanboy of my mother's.

He didn't seem to take much offense, though,

crouching next to me then sinking to the floor, keeping enough distance it wasn't entirely creepy. His cargo shorts hung below his hairy knees, heavy wool socks and dirty steel-toed boots an odd match, the dried and caked dirt on the soles leaving little clumps behind. "You're Petal Morgan. Annette's daughter." He looked just old enough to have maybe known Mom or been part of her life in some way, likely his late forties or early fifties, face prone to jowls and thinning brown hair chasing his hairline back from his wrinkled brow. But there was a kind of innocence to him that had me relenting just enough I didn't tell him to get lost.

Yet. There was still time for rudeness. Always, actually, but only delivered at the perfect, piercing and diabolical moment. Mom taught me that.

"I'm Marlon. Marlon Landon." He stuck his hand out in that awkward way nervous people have when they come face-to-face with a fantasy made flesh. He was in for a big disappointment and I needed to wash my hands. Talk about damp palms, yuck.

Petal, at least *try* to be nice.

"I'm a huge fan of Annette's," he gushed then, like physical contact gave him permission to pour his enthusiasm for my mother all over me. "You look just like her, you know that, right? I'm so excited to see you again."

Again. There was that word. "You knew Mom." Zero enthusiasm mustered, but he didn't notice or let it bother him, carrying on like me speaking was all he needed.

"I was at the house all the time," he said, "parties and stuff. I worked for the studio. I worked on *Lucille*." I knew he meant the movie, not the car. "Your mother was so talented." Yeah, blah blah, dude. "No one knew what happened to you, where you went. There was a rumor about an FBI agent, but that was it." He glanced toward Agent Dune. "Was the rumor right?"

"Yeah," I said, knowing it was dumb to give up personal information but suddenly so tired, weary to the bone and not caring what I said or did, my usual defensiveness fell away and abandoned me. "One of the agents, the one who found me. He adopted me." Carried me away like a white king on a horse and made me his daughter and a princess forever and ever.

I was making myself sick.

"Are you here... did you come to take Lucille home?" He glanced at the curtain. "I bet you'd love to have her."

He bet wrong. "I'm just wrapping up the past, Marlon," I said. "Wanted to say goodbye. You know." Left it at that because dude obviously had a thing for Mom and she was dead so why bother shattering his illusions? I had enough of my own broken I didn't need to do it to a stranger.

He nodded with enthusiasm, the faint scent of BO drifting toward me, one big hand fiddling with the badge hanging from his own lanyard. "It must be so hard to say goodbye." Tears shone in his eyes. "After what happened.

—when he struck her and struck her and she screamed and fell on the bed—

I jerked back from the memory. Hang on a second. I didn't see her fall. I was hiding in the closet. I didn't see anything.

Was my encounter with Agent Dune forcing recall on the past or was this whole situation creating false images to fill in the gaps? I had no clue, but whatever the truth, I wanted off this ride, thanks.

Marlon flinching like I'd lashed out at him. No idea what expression crossed my face to make him react that way, but I was too tired to sort it out. Made a small effort and let it be enough.

"Sorry," I said. "Just tired."

"I have some of her things," he blurted after a moment of uncomfortable silence in which I wished he'd just get up and leave already. "Some clothes, a prop from Lucille." His hopeful expression had me cringing. "If you'd like, I could show them to you sometime."

He had no idea the torture he put me through, sitting there, trying to tell him how horrifying that idea was, how truly and absolutely revolting, that I would rather throw myself off a cliff—

Reggie's return had him scrambling to his feet, my best friend eyeing him up with a scowl he took as his invitation to get the hell out. She didn't even have to speak, just arched one of those perfectly penciled brows at him and Marlon skedaddled. I pulled her down next to me and hugged her, feeling filthy, like even the hottest shower but with bleach was in order and knowing even that would never rinse me clean.

"Reggie," I said. "I want to go home."

She met my eyes, nodded. "Okay, sweet," she said.

When I stood up, I realized I should have gone to the washroom with her. "Where did you find the ladies'?"

She pointed at a sign. "I'll show you."

"All good," I said. "You sit, rest your feet. I'll be right back."

Reggie watched me go and I waved, glancing back a few times so she'd know I knew she was paying attention. Made it to the door to the bathroom but no further, the Israeli man from earlier stepping in my path and stopping me in my tracks.

"Petal Morgan," he said with a huge smile, offering his hand. When I took it, he kissed the back of mine, giving me a shiver down my spine I wasn't sure was a good feeling. "Yosef Moshe, a delight to meet the daughter of Annette Morgan." He looked up and over my shoulder, shrugging. "Or would be more delightful under different circumstances."

"Trust me, Mr. Moshe," I said, "Mom would have found this hilarious."

He hesitated, smile flickering in and out like he wasn't sure if I was joking.

"I see," he said. Carried on like nothing untoward happened while I was the most untoward he would ever meet. "I'm here from Israel, my sole purpose—"

"Let me guess," I cut him off. "Lucille." His nod and return to confusion as if not sure how to deal with me had me sighing. "Listen, I don't own her, I can't help you buy her. She was that guy's," I jabbed a finger in the corpse's direction, hidden behind the curtain or not, "so if you think I can somehow magically help you obtain her, you're deluded."

His face darkened, but his smile remained. "I don't need your assistance in the purchase," he said, voice dropping, "but in another matter entirely."

Okay, he had my attention. "Shoot," I said. "But hurry." I pointed at the sign over the bathroom door.

"There are rumors," he said, "your mother hid a large collection of very expensive jewelry in Lucille."

I'd wanted closure. That meant confronting things I'd stuffed deep, things I'd prefer never saw the light of day. Case in point. I froze, heart pounding, stomach in knots. I knew exactly the jewelry he meant. Could see it in my mind's eye the afternoon the man in the turban and white robes— my young mind didn't know he was a Saudi prince— gave them to her.

Yosef Moshe's impatience got the better of him. "Can you confirm or deny?"

I glared back suddenly, hating he'd triggered that particular recall and wanting to lash back. Almost told him where to go. Didn't. Answered his question instead.

"No," I said. "Mom didn't hide anything in Lucille. Now, if you'll excuse me." I pushed past him and into the bathroom, locking myself in a stall to shake and cry and try to forget while memory refused to let me.

CHAPTER FIVE

AFTER I'D HAD ENOUGH of the sob fest, I finally emerged, checking myself in the mirror, caught by the drawn and weary expression on my face, my bloodshot eyes. But, more than anything, how much I looked like her.

My mother.

I'd won the genetic lottery, that had never been in question. Thick blonde hair, blue eyes, perfect skin, naturally thin and high metabolism that made eating whatever I wanted that hated goal I knew other women envied. Tall but not too tall, just kissing thirty. Classically beautiful, just like her.

My mother.

Jordan had been right to call me selfish and heartless and all those other things he'd thrown at me like emotional hand grenades that seemed to land now stronger than they had when he'd originally lobbed them. I had to fight the shaking and the knots in my stomach, the reminder that PTSD wasn't something I could just get over, that the fact I'd refused therapy might not have been the best option but seemed the only one at the time.

Wow, my fathers. They needed awards for that level of patience.

"Ms. Morgan." Great, another one, though the young Japanese woman Yosef had called Ashe didn't intrude the way he or Marlon had, not quite deferential but present. "My name is Ashe Yoshida. I represent a buyer who wishes to acquire Lucille." She handed me a card. Plain black, with a number in white on the front. That was it. No name, no nothing.

"I'll tell you what I told Mr. Moshe," I said. "I have no way of helping your client get his hands on Lucille." Of course it had to be a man, her client. Only men were that pathetic about Mom.

Ashe inclined her head, her perfect black bob shifting forward in a silky fall, pageboy bangs moving when her long lashes blinked. "He does not need your help to acquire Lucille," she said. Turned and walked away.

"Wait." I held the card out. "What am I supposed to do with this?"

She tilted her head just slightly, face expressionless. "Call the number, Ms. Morgan." And left me alone, though not entirely because a couple of women entered just then, their eyes skimming over me with recognition.

Which meant I bolted, stuffing the card into my pocket and hurrying back to Reggie.

I was almost at her side again when my phone rang, Dad's number making me stop in my tracks. "Hey," I said.

"Petal." He sounded like he was on the move, voice low and intense. "Are you all right?"

I looked up, noticed Agent Dune glancing my way and scowled at her. "She called you."

"Who? No one called me, Pet. Listen to me, I heard about the death. Are you all right?"

"Yes, Dad." I sank down next Reggie. "We're fine. We're just waiting for them to release us."

"Do *not*," he said then, so abruptly and intensely I felt my heart skip, "say a single word to anyone. About anything. Do you hear me? Petal, I mean it. Not a word to Dune or the LAPD until I get there."

Get…? "Dad, what's going on?"

"I'm on my way." He hung up before I could ineffectually demand he answer me, but it didn't matter, because Agent Dune and her partner were on the march and if Dad was warning me to keep my mouth shut?

This couldn't be good.

"Play dumb," I whispered to Reggie as I stood and faced down the advancing agents.

"Um, not hard," she shot back. "Petal, what did you do?"

"I have no idea," I said, "but apparently the FBI thinks something." I nodded to Dune just before she joined us.

"Feeling better, Ms. Morgan?" She outright ignored Reggie this time, but the familiarity and attempt at that weird version of connection was long gone.

"A bit, thanks," I said. "When can we go?"

"After you answer a few questions," she said. "You told me you didn't know the victim, correct?"

I shrugged. "That's what I said." Those were words, Petal. Dad would be pissed. But I couldn't stonewall completely. I needed to know what was going on.

"Interesting," she said. "Then why is it you were texting him?"

Texting? I wasn't texting—

No. *I* wasn't. But I bet I knew who was. That sneaky, conniving… hope you find what you're looking for, my ass.

I was going to kill the Chameleon the next chance I got.

CHAPTER SIX

REGGIE MOVED FASTER THAN my alcohol influenced brain. While I pondered the means I had at my disposal to end the life of the woman I had zero doubt set me up, my bestie stepped between me and the FBI agent now looking at me like a suspect with her expression not just flat but downright hostile.

"You can ask all the questions you like," she said. "But Petal won't be saying a word without her lawyer present."

Dune shrugged. "Fine. Why don't we all go somewhere more official and have a conversation there." Threatening enough for you? I knew exactly what that meant, that I was about to sit in an interrogation room for several hours or as long as they wanted to keep me under wraps and uncomfortable while Reggie wrangled legal counsel and I continued to plot the death and destruction of someone I never should have trusted in the first place.

Oh, yes, this trip had been the best idea I'd ever had.

"I had nothing to do with that man's death." I hadn't meant to speak out loud, Reggie turning to hiss at me, but my statement opened up the door to Agent Dune and her line of questioning, so it was my own fault, really.

"Then why did you offer to show Edison Fisher where your mother hid the missing jewelry everyone seems to think is in that car?" She pointed at the velvet curtain without taking her eyes off me.

I finally learned to shut my mouth, though I did shake my head. And followed just as silently, Reggie at my side, as the two FBI agents escorted me out of the ballroom.

Whatever game the Chameleon was playing, had played with me in the past, things just got real. Though, I had no idea why or what her motivation might be for setting me up for murder.

But, trust me. I'd be finding out, right before she breathed her last breath.

Remember I mentioned the whole interrogation room thing? Yeah, that happened. Agent Dune separated me from Reggie when we arrived at the LAPD precinct, my bestie already on the phone after whispering to me one more time not to say a word. Considering she was the daughter of a well-known and, as of yet, innocent until proven guilty head of an organized crime family, my best friend was probably the perfect person to have on my side. Not that Reggie engaged in the family business, to the contrary. She'd bought Full Reveal and the After Hours Club as her way of defying her father and being her own boss. Were both establishments completely on the up-and-up? I had no idea and didn't care because it was none of my beeswax. And I hardly had the moral and ethical fortitude to judge her for the choices she made. I'd taken what amounted to at least lightly soiled money as my first payment from her and had been employed by friends of hers I certainly couldn't call completely honest in their own entrepreneurial pursuits. None of the people I'd worked with were as fresh as morning daisies, not even Detective Elle Gordon's beloved auntie, Valentina June, the medium who regularly took money from people as part of an acceptable fraud scam practiced the world over.

All that aside, while I settled into the hard metal chair at the hard metal table in the dingy room with the one-way mirror, I crossed my arms over my chest and closed my eyes against the headache now fully formed behind my temples. I couldn't just blame the overindulgence that had me tipsy earlier, either. Stress and lack of sleep not to mention the almost endless overlay of flickering memory had me clenching my jaw so tight the pain in my head increased exponentially.

Did this to myself? Guilty on all charges, your honor.

I hated not knowing what was going on, no clock in the room, my phone confiscated. I hoped they'd overstep and search it because when they did they'd find zilcho to back up the ridiculous claim I'd been talking with Edison Fisher.

That was, as long as the Chameleon didn't pull a fast one and somehow rig my messages. My confidence eroded quickly after I allowed myself that particular line of thought, though I did my best to hide it. Fidgeting would only suggest guilt, so I drew on Dad and Elle and every stoic everyone in my life (looking at you, Rafael Van Dorn) to fortify me, holding as still and quiet as I could, closing my eyes against the pain, though doing that allowed memories to surface, to take control. The old ones no longer completely trustworthy, the new ones I'd had claw their way to the top of the pile no more believable. All of which mashed together into a quickly unbearable state of affairs that forced my eyes open so I could pretend I wasn't losing my marbles.

Staring at whoever it was waiting and watched on the other side of the glass would have to do.

That and kicking myself for ever believing the Chameleon meant me anything but harm. What was I thinking? I wasn't. I was reacting and I'd played right into whatever scheme it was she'd set me up for.

Now, I had zero reason to believe this would end in me doing time. I hadn't killed Edison Fisher, there was no proof I had. Every attempt my brain made to suggest she might frame me right down to putting me in an orange jumpsuit for a crime I didn't commit ended in doubt. Not that I didn't think she was capable, but we just didn't have that kind of relationship. I wanted to believe that, anyway. So, I let myself settle and believe while she may have orchestrated this to get me out of the way while she completed whatever assignment she'd taken this time, I knew I'd be vindicated and released to pursue her another day.

It wasn't helping I knew Dad was on the way, shoved that fact to the back of my mind and smothered it in resentment. I didn't need him to run to my rescue. I was perfectly capable of not just getting myself into trouble, but out of it as well. The reminder of my childhood in California, the renewal of old hurts long buried just as deep but surfacing thanks to this mess, only increased my tension and anger. Yes, I'd needed him then. Yes, he'd made me feel safe for the first time in my life and I'd clung to him, wept on his shoulder, played victim. I was eight freaking years old.

That was a long time ago and I wasn't a victim anymore. I wouldn't be climbing out of a pile of clothes scented heavily with my mother's perfume after listening to her husband beat her to death to cling to the White King FBI God who lifted me out of the dark and held me. Not this time.

Not ever again.

The fact none of this was Dad's fault and he really had saved me from a wretched future in foster care and devolution likely to drugs or some other addiction instead of giving me a lovely and loving life fell to the wayside while I glared at the glass hard enough I had to finally blink and look away.

Down at my hands, now fallen to my lap, clenched. And had an epiphany.

This really *wasn't* about Lucille. I'd been telling the truth all along while not completely believing it. Until now. At least, it wasn't for *her*, the Chameleon, even if I still fought off the hate I felt for the dumb car. God, I was such an idiot. I almost laughed out loud in angry realization, a barking sound I had to clip at the source, only allowing a residual grunt to escape. It had been in front of me all along. Of course I knew what the Chameleon was after, why she'd lured me out here to California, to that wretched car and the memories that haunted me.

The jewelry. She wanted Mom's missing jewelry. And she thought I knew how to find it.

I did grin then, a tight and furious expression I hoped Agent Dune caught and tried to fathom because she had no idea. None. No one did. Though the rumor persisted, I knew for a fact my mother had never hidden anything of value in Lucille. And that was the funniest and most horrific part of all of this. I'd been dragged back into Mom's drama and my own hurt for someone else's desire for gain.

How delightful the Chameleon would end up

disappointed again. Almost worth the frame job.

The door opened, after how long I had no idea. One thing about being lost in your past due to untreated mental trauma, time flew when you let it take you over. I looked up, back in the present in a flash but startled and out of sorts long enough I gaped at the person who joined me at the table, instead of hiding my surprise as I should have done.

"Ms. Morgan," Ashe Yoshida said, her dark bob and pageboy bangs still perfect around her lovely face, "I'm sorry for the delay." She looked up then, same empty expression focusing on Agent Dune who scowled at me from the doorway. "I hope you haven't mistreated my client, agent," she said. "Now, if you'll excuse us, I need to speak with her. Alone." She gestured at the camera in the corner, the red light blinking out before nodding at the exit.

Agent Dune left, visibly reluctant, while I gaped at the young woman who'd handed me the black business card in the bathroom at the auction. She sat next to me in a smooth motion, dark suit pristine while I was sure I looked like someone dragged me here rather than drove me across town in the back seat of a cruiser.

"Apologies for the delay," she said. "My employer didn't realize you'd been brought in for questioning. I'm offering my services." She handed me a new card, this one with her name and number on it, the white backing less ominous. "I have no doubt you are innocent, Ms. Morgan. If you'll allow me, I'll make arrangements for your release." She stood just as quickly as she'd sat down, heading for the door. No waiting, all assumptions, though I wasn't about to argue if she had a plan. "I'll be right back."

CHAPTER SEVEN

S HE RETURNED, GOOD TO her word, Agent Dune on her heels, a tall, scruffy looking detective at her side, the used-to-be handsome man with his graying three day beard and wrinkled suit standing against the wall instead of coming to sit with us, his intensely blue eyes focused on me while Ashe turned to face down Dune with that impeccable emptiness I was beginning to think meant she was some kind of automaton and not a human being at all.

"Your attempt to uncover evidence against my client has gained you nothing," Ashe said. "The text messages you claim came from Ms. Morgan were, in fact, a ruse carried out by some other party via an untraceable phone."

"A burner she could be concealing," Dune said.

"A burner you have failed to uncover despite

your illegal search of Ms. Morgan's things in her hotel room." The agent flinched, glanced at the man watching before returning her focus to me.

"I apologize for the over eager attentions of the LAPD in this matter," Dune said.

"Not to mention further apology to Ms. Morgan for holding her here without cause." Ashe motioned for me to rise. "Since her cell phone has no evidence whatsoever of any conversation with Mr. Fisher aside from the photograph of him in her mother's car, as she originally offered," I nodded at that, "not to mention said conversation offers zero implication of impending death, lacking any threat of personal or bodily harm, regardless of the source of that conversation or who might be impersonating my client, you have nothing. And you know it." Not a challenge, just pure and logical fact. "Now, that said and without any further reason for you to hold her, I'm taking my client with me, Agent Dune, Detective Miller." So, he was LAPD. That made sense. "Ms. Morgan." Ashe headed for the door without further ado, Dune's frown of frustration rather satisfying.

Before we managed to exit, the agent spoke up, forcing me to pause in line with the tall detective who stared down at me with a smirk, though without the accusation in his face I'd been expecting. Was that curiosity? Didn't matter, not when Dune cut through the triumphant exit with her need to have the last word.

"Don't leave LA, Ms. Morgan," she said. "We'll have more questions for you."

"All of which," Ashe said, "you will direct through me, Agent Dune." She nodded to the man. "Detective Miller." Strode out as though she owned the place with me on her heels.

I kept moving when she did, walking through the precinct bullpen at a steady stride, not hurrying but finding I had to push myself to keep up with Ashe. I'd been in places like this before, not just thanks to the work I did and the bodies I'd found, but when I was a little girl, so the stares and whispers and suppositions were all familiar enough it didn't bother me being the center of their attention and likely judgements. Whatever. They could keep their guesswork and shove it.

It wasn't until we reached the elevator and the doors closed behind us I exhaled the tension that held my headache in place, feeling that pain ease somewhat, reduced to a dull throb behind my eyes. "Thanks for that," I said.

"My employer is more than happy to assist," she said. Exited the elevator and kept moving while I hesitated as she stopped at the side desk and signed for a bag, handing me my things. Not much, my cell, my wallet, the black card she'd given me, my lanyard and badge. I took the plastic in my hands, staring down at the sum total of my possessions while she marched off again. I let her go, except that wasn't on her agenda, was it? She stopped and turned back, staring at me with that expressionlessness that made goosebumps rise on my arms. "This way, Ms. Morgan."

Yeah, um, nope. "I need to find my friend." No way was I leaving without finding Reggie. She had to be here still. She wouldn't have just left.

"Ms. Nolan is presently on her way to the airport," she said, "to pick up those who have come to your rescue." Dad, right. Wait, those? That implied more than just my specifically stupendous special agent father. Who else was on that plane? "Since we have time, my employer would request you join him for a conversation." Didn't *sound* like a request.

"He wants something for helping me, is that it?" Not sure I had anything to give. And I didn't just mean tangible anything. I was out of juice and patience and wanted to go back to the hotel and pack and get the heck out of LA no matter what Dune said.

"No strings." Ashe stood there, expectation in her nothingness. "Just a talk." She gestured at the exit. "A short talk."

I debated walking away, leaving her and her robot-like personality in my dust. But her boss had gotten me out of the mess I'd been in pretty efficiently, so if he wanted a short talk? Done. Except he might not like what he heard if he pushed me, because I was in the mood to hand over an earful.

The limo waiting for us shouldn't have surprised me, nor the fact Ashe instantly focused all her attention on her own phone when we settled in the back seat and the driver pulled away without having to be told where to go. Okay then. That gave me time to text Reggie, at least, noting the security features on my phone had been disabled. FBI tech jerks. Not like I had hard-core protections or anything, just a silly four-digit passcode. But they could have at least pretended they hadn't hacked me.

I'm out, I sent. *You're getting Dad?*

GIRL. She sent that instantly back. *What happened? I was going to get a lawyer but Simone texted she was on the plane with Andy and to hold off. You okay?*

Simone? What was she doing? *I'm fine*, I sent. Lied. *One of the bidders on Lucille sent his creepy henchwoman.* I thought about sneaking a photo for Reggie's benefit but decided against it. Ashe had the look of someone who could take me apart with her bare hands while sipping tea and crushing a grandmaster at chess. Not pushing my luck unless I had to. *I'm on my way to have a chat with him now. I'll meet you at the hotel.*

Is that safe? She fired off another text before I could respond. *Never mind. Just watch your back. See you soon.* Another pause. *Love you, Petal. We got this.*

I fired off a heart emoji and settled back into the leather seat, staring out the window as LA flashed by. Got lost in my memories again, my anger toward the Chameleon, only emerging when I realized we had left city limits and were climbing into the hills.

It had been a very long time since I'd overlooked LA from this vantagepoint, since I'd lived in a mansion sprawling over its own hilltop, since I'd been a caged princess treated like a toy (when I wasn't ignored or neglected or humiliated) and an inconvenience.

I hated the Hollywood Hills. Felt the gut punch as the limo turned onto a familiar road, up a despised long drive, clenched my entire being into a knot against the understanding I knew exactly where we were headed, where we'd already arrived.

The black car stopped at the top of the driveway, the white house outside the window the very last place in the world I wanted to be.

—endless cars pulling up to the front sweep of steps, the ostentatious white mansion with its sprawling mid-century architecture and overdone landscaping squatting over a view of the shining lights of the distant city, men and women in fancy clothes with their fake smiles and harsh laughter and need to be seen an endless string of nights spent hiding from the crowds of strangers who cared nothing for me and only wanted to be seen, adored, noticed—

I swallowed the bile that rose, the image of the house I knew overlaying the obvious construction happening to my mother's mansion, my hand reaching for the door far too slow, someone on the outside appearing through the tinted glass, pulling it open for me.

I couldn't stop staring, renovations dismantling part of the house I'd never really thought of as home, landscaping scraped to the dull earth of the hillside, the chain-link fence surrounding the property making it feel more like a prison than it had when I was a child.

Gaping felt like a failure, staring just a betrayal of who I'd fought to become. But I couldn't help myself, nor the continuing memories of how it used to be once upon a time that tried to intrude on the reality of what it was *right now*. How to reconcile the hard-hat wearing workmen with the handsome ones in tuxedoes who tried to intrude? Or the beeping of a skid loader backing up to take another run at a pile of dirt compared to a low-slung Lamborghini rumbling to a stop? I blinked several times, swallowing again, knowing I was shaking and unable to stop the reaction despite hugging myself very hard.

"I'm sorry to meet this way," a voice said. Deep, kind, caring even. Cultured, a big hand reaching out, intruding on the memories. Reminding me of another large man with a baritone voice whose compassion had saved me once upon a time and, whether I liked it or not, rode to my rescue even now.

Which meant I welcomed the distraction, turning into the sun, forced to squint until this new so-called savior stepped into the path of it, silhouetted a moment until my eyes adjusted and focused on his facc.

Gorgeous, this man, broad shouldered and fit despite his age, well into his sixties if I had to guess, white hair perfectly styled, blue eyes rimmed in thick lashes, broad jaw tanned and beardless, full lips pulling back into a welcoming smile. The scent of him reached me next, faint breeze carrying it as he stepped closer, that big hand still extended, the cuffs of his white shirt folded to his elbows, collar open to the third button, tan extending beneath.

I knew that scent. Where had I smelled it before? The rest of him I absorbed as I shook his hand at last, the firm grip lingering a moment, other hand tucked into the back pocket of his jeans, that smile never fading.

"Do I know you?" The faint tremor in my voice had me snapping into rigidity because no way was I letting myself fall into darkness in front of who was, for all intents and purposes, a stranger even if he thought he knew me once. The uncertainty and deception of the memories I'd already been dealing with only compounded my anxiety I might trigger a deeper flash into something I wasn't ready to face. Not now, not here. Not ever. "You knew my mother." That came out like an accusation when my overreaction whipped me around to the opposite of my initial question. Anger seemed a solid antidote to my mind's bubbling cauldron of drowned recall so I used it.

He didn't seem to mind, nodded. "Petal," he said. Paused and sighed deeply, releasing my hand. "Roman Sebastian. And yes, I knew your mother, Petal." There was more and I shied from it because I knew what I was here for, didn't I? What he had to say, in a blooming understanding that had panic hit me in a wave of hysteria. But instead of breaking down and blubbering or falling to my knees or snapping completely in half as I feared I would, I found myself standing tall, silent and immobile, as though part of me lifted free to observe with the same detachment Ashe practiced. Not on purpose, without my consent, though I was grateful for the distance as the handsome man who knew my mother—who knew her intimately—went on. "You must think me an old fool," he said, that lovely voice calming despite everything, despite the terror of having to face what he was going to tell me. "Wanting pieces of her after all this time." He looked away and suddenly I could breathe again, though when he gestured at the house and the ongoing work to it, I caught air again, held it. "Obsessed, some call me. But I have my reasons." He looked back to me, so gentle, so hopeful, sadness there too, and ancient grief I understood far more than he would ever know. "I had no idea, Petal. All the times I visited, that I saw you, dismissed you. Forgive me." So much grief. "I swear to you, if I knew who you were... things would have turned out so much differently for you."

I wanted to open my mouth and tell him to stop talking. To turn and run away or start humming with my hands over my ears because this wasn't happening and it couldn't happen and why was he still speaking? Instead, that comforting partition that held my consciousness in its gentle embrace contained any protest. Not grateful for it anymore.

Too late anyway.

"You didn't send me the paternity test, did you?" His smile had a charisma to it, his entire being did, that held me there, trapped by his sorrow and compassion. "I thought it might have been you, at first, but Ashe's investigation told me you had no idea who I was." He spread his hands in front of him, between us. "Who you are to me."

I couldn't even manage to shake my head.

Again, didn't matter.

Roman Sebastian reached up with both big hands and cupped my face, sighing over me. "I see her in you," he said. "You are your mother, Petal. But you're me, too. My daughter. Aren't you?"

CHAPTER EIGHT

I HAD TWO CHOICES in that moment. Go full gush and hug him and cry and be all Daddy's girl come home, happily ever after, fairytale ending of the century epic meltdown to a classic Hollywood fade to black.

Or.

I don't even have to identify *or*, right? You know which one I picked.

With every single ounce of Andrew Freaking Walker, FBFreakingI wrapped around me like a cloak, Detective Elle SuperHeroine Gordon zipped up the back and Regina Take-No-Crap Nolan clamped down over my head like a helmet, I held onto me—Petal Screw-Up-Central Morgan, at your service—and refused to crumble.

Refused to sway.

Re-heckno-fused to be that girl.

"Let me guess," I said, succeeding at sounding bored, cold, unimpressed. Go me. "You received the test from an anonymous source." Chameleon, another one I owed you. "And you believed it."

Roman nodded, drew a little breath before responding, though his open emotion didn't shift despite the wall of my denial and rejection.

"I did," he said. "And had it retested, just to be sure."

"How exactly did you get your hands on my DNA?" Creep. More reason to step back from this, to run from it. But I didn't, boo-yah.

"I used your mother's," he said, blue eyes suddenly anxious, shaking his head. "Not yours, Petal. While not entirely accurate, it confirmed enough matching markers. With your consent, I'd like to do an actual test with a contribution from you, but I'm satisfied Annette and I are your biological parents."

Satisfied, was he? Good for him.

Roman's continuing softness disarmed me as much as anything, though I wasn't going to let myself go just because the man might or might not have been (was, come on, Petal) my sperm donor.

"I was hoping." He stopped before finishing the thought then rushed on. "Would you like to take a stroll? See what changes I'm making?"

"I would rather gouge out my eyes with a spoon," I said. Felt myself begin to tremble, the armor I wore failing me. Not because the people who made it up were weak. No, because *I* was and the courage and power I drew from all they'd taught me could only do so much.

My flaws, my broken pieces. It was a testament to their awesomeness I could even pretend to be like them at all.

I waved off the horrible thing I'd said with a tsking sound, looking away from those blue eyes, to the pathway the construction crew left around the outside of the main renovation area and, without asking if he wanted to join me, headed out on a walkabout of my mother's old house, hearing his crunching footsteps following me while I hugged myself tight and glared at the memories still invading my mind.

Clearly I needed to be medicated.

"I'm sorry it had to happen this way." His words were almost lost in the booming sound of a piece of sheet metal dropping to the ground, Roman moving to the inside, what, to protect me? Whatever his reason, his body blocked most of the dust that drifted toward us. I stared at the ugly ground and let him speak. Just to get it over with. "I never expected... Petal, I'm not asking for you to accept me. I only need you to hear me out."

I chose silence as acquiescence and he took it for what it meant.

"I met your mother so long ago, but she's still with me, you know." His sadness had humor in it, though I refused to look at him again. "I dabbled at being a producer back then. It's how we met." A deep sigh followed. "She thought it was funny, teased me about wasting my money on movies. She was right. I had terrible taste in scripts, but not in her." If he said so. I begged to differ. "Annette would have appreciated the fact I took her advice and moved on. Venture capitalism suits me better, I think, among other things. Though, I'm glad I at least had the chance to know her. Even if it cost me." He chuckled. "More than money. It cost me my heart."

I stopped abruptly, unable to keep quiet any longer. "She wasn't the woman you thought she was." Why didn't anyone see that? I hadn't meant to raise my voice, to let my rage out, but it came anyway, with the words, pouring forth like lava too long contained inside. "She was a horrible, narcissistic and abusive child who treated everyone around her like crap."

He nodded slowly. "I know, Petal," he said.

Wait, what? "And you still love her?" I thought there was something wrong with me. This guy was the real idiot.

Roman looked out over the crest of the hill at LA, breeze ruffling his white hair, the collar of his shirt. "I saw Annette's shortcomings. But there was a beautiful young woman inside her, a tortured soul, who showed up so infrequently. When she did, Petal…" He met my eyes again. "When she did, I believed anything was possible. Including saving her."

I would not let him and his dumb ass hormonal, heroic freaking savior complex manly-manness erase one iota of the resentment and anger I still held toward my mother. He had no idea. None.

None.

"She taught me better," he said, strolling on, forcing me to follow, which I did despite not caring what he had to say while suddenly caring very much. "Drove me away with all the tools she had at her disposal. Lured me back with promises she'd never keep. I had no illusions, not really, that she'd leave Daniel." I flinched. Erased her husband's name from my mind after her death, after he killed her. More memories I was forced to face. "All while my heart broke knowing if I'd just gotten to her sooner, tried harder, I might have been able to save her."

"You knew all along she was married." That was meant to hurt, to wound, to cut. He deserved to suffer, didn't he? He was making me suffer, so he needed to feel the pain I felt if this ridiculous conversation was going to continue. "You know what that makes you, right?"

Roman's flash of a smile told me he took no offense. "I was rather… known for my unwillingness to honor the bonds of matrimony back in the day." He laughed, rueful but unapologetic. "And the nights we spent together were Annette's idea. Not that I even considered turning her down."

"How trite," I snapped. "And pathetic, really. If you'd just been more careful I wouldn't have to be standing here having this conversation, would I?" Nope. I wouldn't even have existed. Take that and chew on it, little girl.

He shrugged then, expression falling into that

seemingly bottomless compassion again. "Not the first time it happened, I've come to discover. You're not my only daughter, Petal." Oh, great. Not only was he a dog, he had more kids?

Took me a second.

To understand the implications.

To catch my breath.

While Roman turned to me one last time, hands catching my upper arms, drawing me close. "If I had known about you." Tears welled in his blue eyes. "I would have done everything in my power to protect you. Given you the life she couldn't. Petal, I would have saved you."

I jerked free of his touch, flatlining my own emotions again. Shoving aside the understanding that almost unhinged my control. I should have thanked him for giving me what I needed to push back the emotions threatening to take me over. "But you weren't there and you didn't save me," I snarled. "Someone else did that for you. Oh, and just so you know? I don't need you to save me now, Roman. In case you missed it, I'm perfectly capable of doing that myself."

"You are remarkable," he said then, voice soft. Nothing I said or did seemed to ruffle him, to break through his kindness, his old grief. "I'm hardly surprised. And yes, I looked into you, I know who you've become. And who it was that helped shape you. Two incredible parents, both of whom I respect very much. Your brother, as well, an extraordinary young man. Petal, I don't want to take you away from that, or erase any of the good they did. I know they are your family. I just want a chance to be part of that in whatever small way you're willing to consider."

I couldn't. I just... *couldn't.* My chest hurt and my stomach clenched and I couldn't breathe or speak or think or feel—

Couldn't.

I spun away from him and almost ran back down the path, finally fleeing from him, from my past and the reawakened agony of all that was the disaster of my brilliant idea to come to LA, to find closure. Instead reopening old wounds and letting them gape and bleed and choke off my ability to pretend I was okay.

Not broken.

Nice try at being normal, Petal Morgan.

I never noticed if he followed me and somehow ended up in the back seat of the limo all over again, panting and clenching in the tears and screams that threatened to emerge if I wasn't allowed to leave right freaking now already.

He wasn't ready to let me go just yet, looming in the opening of the door, voice very low and soft as his attempt to be unthreatening and continue this charade of caring he seemed to think was helping his case only made things worse. "Your sister is in town," he said. "She wants the three of us to meet. If you're up to it…"

I reached out and grabbed the door handle, pulling it shut. He stepped back just in time to not get himself slammed in it when I jerked it closed.

Stared down at my feet as the car circled the drive, back seat beside me squeaking just a little, leather giving way as the other person in the car shifted slightly.

Ashe. I'd forgotten she was there. Hoped she'd keep her silence as she had on the way to the house. Fell into misery when she complied, distant and uncaring as ever as I bit my lower lip hard to keep from weeping like the broken child I had always been.

CHAPTER NINE

I BARELY REMEMBERED THE drive, probably a good thing, though when the limo pulled up outside my hotel, I had an uncomfortable moment that Roman Sebastian knew where I was staying. Heck, if the woman sitting next to me who finally looked up from her phone was as good as I thought she was… too late. Hadn't he already proven he knew everything else about me, too?

Ashe met my eyes with her own dark ones. "You have his number," she said. "It's his direct line. He wants you to know you can call him at any time, for any reason, day or night."

The temptation to pull out the card and shred it in front of her was so strong (and so childish) I had to breathe a moment and not move to keep it from becoming reality. Finally on the edge of control again, I shoved open the limo door to the startled expression of the driver who'd come to let me out and stomped my way through the glass doors of the Hollywood Haven Hotel.

Kept stomping, all the way to the elevator which I waited for in impatient anger, ignoring the happy couple and staring little girl who seemed nervous of my temper. Way to freak out a random kid, Petal. Still wasn't enough to pull me back from the brink of yelling and throwing things and punching pillows.

My exact plan, as a matter of fact, the moment I arrived in my room. Which took far too long, thank you. I pressed the keycard to the lock, grimacing when it took two tries to get a green light, all my focus on getting inside, grabbing a pillow and screaming my head off until I passed out.

Yeah, that didn't get to happen. Because the second I stepped through and into the suite Reggie and I shared I was ambushed by hugging people who demanded to know if I was okay (Dad), if anyone needed to be arrested, (Simone) or if there was anything I needed to tell them (thanks a lot for that, Elle). My surprise the detective had joined Simone and Dad on the flight out to California saved them all from previously required shouting, but only barely.

"What," I snapped at the three of them, "are you even doing here?"

I knew why Dad had come, of course. Simone Evans, on the other hand, while someone I considered a good friend despite the fact she was the girlfriend of my ex-husband, should have left her butt in DC.

"You needed a good lawyer," she said, dark eyes determined, dressed casually in jeans and a T-shirt, likely for the flight, but ready for a fight, I was sure.

"They have lawyers in LA, Simone." Gracious, wasn't I? I fixed Elle Gordon with my next stink-eye. "And they have detectives here too, just in case you didn't know that."

"I do know that," she said with her typical level and uncompromising stare that didn't judge so much as it calmed. But I didn't want to be calm right now, damn it. "In fact, that's why I came. I used to *be* one of those detectives."

Wait, she'd worked in LA? I brushed off the excuse, tossing my hands, catching Reggie's wince as I took out the last few hours on the people who loved me.

"I'm fine. Go home. I'll be on the next flight myself. I'm done with this stupid idea and I can't wait to put it behind me." Took a long, deep breath, at least tried for thankful. "I know why you're here and I love you for it. But I don't need rescuing. I didn't do anything wrong. And as soon as I can rearview mirror this entire scenario, we can all go back to pretending I'm not broken."

"Pet," Dad said. Cleared his throat. "You can't leave."

Like hecking feck. "Watch me."

"Petal." Simone reached for me, hand brushing my arm. "The FBI." She glanced at Dad, back to me.

"Don't be an idiot," Elle said then in smooth alto. "You're not going anywhere until the authorities say you can."

Oh. Right. Well, craptastic on a crapstick.

I met Dad's eyes, felt a tiny thread of nervousness crack through the simmering anger, finally cool me off sufficiently I was able to ask the obvious question. "What are you worried about? Dad, I didn't kill anyone."

"I know that, Pet," he said instantly, so at least he hadn't added murder suspect to his list of things Petal did to make him crazy. I had my own list about him, so it was all good. "I spoke to Celia. She seems to think she'll have enough evidence to…" he stopped then hurried on, "ask you more questions shortly."

Yeah, not what he meant to say. "She thinks she has something on me?" What? Had I again given the Chameleon too much credit talking myself down from thinking she wasn't trying to put me in prison?

"I can't protect you." Dad sounded defeated. Looked it, too, face pale, normally FBI stoicness suffering under the weight of what I was doing to him. Yes, I took full responsibility even if I couldn't bring myself to cross to him and hug him to at least make an effort at reconciliation. "I'm sorry, Petal. I can't interfere."

"*I* can." Dad might have had rules to follow but Elle didn't seem to think they applied to her. Her gray eyes held me as she tossed her blonde ponytail, still dressed as she always was in her button up and jeans, dress jacket and boots, to the point I wondered if she slept in them, too. "Let me do some digging." She turned to Dad. "I figure you have some Bureau friends you might be able to invite for coffee, Andy?"

He hesitated then nodded. "Coffee, right," he said. "Of course." That seemed to retract the claws of fear he'd been showing, his natural state returning in a visible uplift of his chin and shoulders until the man I'd always admired—and who made me wish was my real dad (he was, but you know)—let my friend's attempt at consolation win. Took a fellow law enforcement officer to do it, though.

"Meanwhile, I'll see what other evidence she thinks she has," Simone said. Paused, shifted into a more professional demeanor. "I was told you had counsel? I'm happy to advise whoever it was you hired."

She better not have her nose out of joint, because the last person I wanted representing me was Ashe Yoshida. I shook my head. "Never mind her," I said. "Thanks, Simone." I drew a breath. "Thanks, all of you." I really should have been more grateful from the get-go. "It's all going to work out."

Shouldn't it have been my loved ones offering such consolation? Whatever, not like my life wasn't the twisty-turny, upsidedowny and insideouty kind anyway. Clearly they were all accustomed to the fact things would not, in fact, work out. At least, not right away. That would be too easy and not my MO at all.

"Petal," Simone said then, "we can at least clarify one point Agent Dune brought up. Can you tell us where you were last night?"

"Here," I said, nodding to Reggie who flinched again. Wait, what? "We flew in, landed about 7PM local. Limo ride over, that's it. I was with Reggie all evening, right?" She nodded at that. "Then we went to bed." Oh, whoops. I wasn't here all night. "I went to the gym," I said. "For a run." Insomnia meant hitting the treadmill because I wasn't interested in sleeping pills.

Simone sighed, nodded. "In the middle of the night."

"Let me guess," I said. "TOD?"

"Midnight," Elle said, almost cheerful. "How was your run, Petal?"

CHAPTER TEN

S PEAK OF THE DEVIL, I'd barely comprehended the implications of what Elle found so amusing when someone knocked firmly on the door. At least they didn't come busting inside, though Agent Celia Dune looked like that would have been her preference. As for the detective who joined her, I wondered at the fact she'd come with one of LAPD's finest (that was a stretch) and not her own partner but didn't seem to be part of the point so I let it go in favor of scowling at the two and holding ground.

Not letting them in. Because I was petty that way and I'd already endured enough, thanks, so they could sod off.

Except my father was much more a gentleman and joined me, gently guiding me to one side, Simone and Elle filling the entry with bodies, Reggie lurking behind them.

"Celia," Dad said, nodding to his fellow agent.

Her frown deepened at the sight of him. "You were warned not to interfere, Andy."

Dad's normally calm exterior cracked enough he shot her a scowl in return. "I don't see how coming to support my daughter who's being questioned in a murder investigation is interfering. Unless there's some wrongdoing on your part I should know about? Mishandling of this case won't look good on your record, Celia. Or make you a star if you succeed in proving an innocent woman guilty because you can't see past your own ambitions."

Turned out Dad knew her very well then, right?

"Not to mention the misconduct of the LAPD so far," Simone chimed in, all litigation queen all the time. "The illegal search of this room and Ms. Morgan's property won't look good to a judge or either of your bosses, I assure you."

Agent Dune drew an angry breath, Dad squaring off to go to battle, while the LAPD detective—Ashe had called him Miller, I think—chuckled.

Well, that was unexpected and disarming enough to settle down the battle before it really got going. Elle reached out one hand and shook his, her grin a match.

"Hey, Pete," she said. "You look like crap."

"Elle," he said, "honest as ever." He ran one hand over his hair, messing it further, making no effort to straighten himself out. While there was a feral feel to the detective, he had an odd personality to him and the same sort of appealing charisma I'd experienced from Roman Sebastian that had me relaxing just a little.

Until I realized I'd drawn a parallel I didn't want to think about because it meant my sperm donor left an impression on me and tensed all over again.

Agent Dune seemed unhappy the pair knew one another. "Detective Gordon," she said. "You're out of your jurisdiction."

"Just here for moral support, Agent Dune," Elle said in that affable and yet completely composed and professional way of hers that put others at ease but told me she had zero respect for the agent in question. "Petal's not just a good friend, but a consultant for my department." Chew on that, Dune. "So naturally my captain and myself have an interest in how this all goes down." She shrugged, all nonchalance and yet brimming with warning. "I have no desire to interfere either, but Petal deserves the very best both of your organizations have to offer when it comes to investigating this terrible tragedy."

I could have hugged her, wanted to grin, felt the expression fight for space on my face and had to look down because despite my temper tantrum still unrequited and my lingering hurt and the triggering memories I batted at like ghosts, leave it to Elle Gordon to make me laugh.

"Sounds good to me," Detective Pete Miller said, nodding to me. "Let's get to the deets, shall we?" I stuck out my chin but didn't argue. "I take it you have an excellent reason for being in the lobby and near the event entry last night at midnight?"

Security cameras. Surely they vindicated me. This whole conversation should have been proof, my alibi, not the accusation I was now guessing it to be. "I went for a run," I said. "Couldn't sleep. In case you forgot, Agent Dune, I already told you why I'm here. For closure. I was contacted with that photo you found on my phone, a fact I was totally up front about. The individual who sent it told me Lucille was up for auction. All I wanted was to come to California and say goodbye to my murdered mother. I had no reason to kill anyone, especially the man who owned her car."

Dune was about to speak when Miller interrupted.

"The security footage certainly shows you heading in that direction, Ms. Morgan," he said.

"As would the cameras in the gym," I said. "So check them and then go find the killer."

He tsked, shaking his head, regret on his face not reaching those eyes and I realized then here was the smarter and more cunning of the two. "Turns out those cameras weren't working, sadly," he said. "Which means there's no way to corroborate your story."

"Right," I snapped back, while Elle's barest headshake tried to silence me. But I was furious now, because this was ridiculous and if it didn't end soon I was going to explode. "Because I somehow knew the cameras in the gym weren't working and used that diabolical knowledge in my master plan to murder someone over a car I don't even want in the first place." I snorted. "Brilliant deduction, detective, agent. Where'd you two get your badges again? Cereal boxes?"

Miller's eyes narrowed, Dune jumping in.

"You could have tampered with the footage," she said. Stopped herself, likely realizing how stupid that sounded.

"Sure," I said. "Let's break this down, then, shall we? I flew to California with a witness," I jabbed a finger at Reggie, "openly bought a ticket to the convention," okay, so I used a fake name, but this was no time to quibble, "did nothing to hide my intentions from law enforcement and shared all the details of my reasons for being here. Oh, meanwhile I connived to convince hotel security to let me into their video feed, shut down their cameras in the gym, go for a very sweaty run and kill someone over a car I always hated before coming back upstairs." I looked back and forth between them, knowing I needed to stop talking, Simone hissing at me to do so, Dad with his hand on my arm, but I wasn't done. "Check the elevator footage on my way back up. If I don't look like I was running my heart out, arrest me right now."

It was Miller who answered that. But with a question. "What were you running from, Ms. Morgan?"

"Memories, Detective Miller," I said. "Of being a little girl trapped and alone in her mother's closet while the man she thought was her father beat her mother." I paused for effect. "To death."

Both Dune and Miller looked uncomfortable enough at that I figured they were at least partially human.

"We're forgetting the best part," I wrapped up my tirade. "I did all of the aforementioned and then, instead of fleeing LA, attended the very event the dead man made his debut. Because I'm that amazing of a murderer." I glared back and forth between them. "About as good as you two are investigators."

"Petal," Dad said, ever so softly. "That's enough."

"Agreed," Elle grinned. "I think they get the point."

"Petal has answered your questions," Simone said in obvious irritation I'd done so, "and unless you have something that actually ties her to the murder, I'm going to ask you both to leave. Now."

"Who sent you that photo, Ms. Morgan?" Again with Captain Cleverpants. Miller glanced at Elle who now stood stone faced, Dad, too. While I tossed caution to the wind despite the people I cared about, because honestly? They might have cared about me, and vice versa. But I was past caring about myself right now.

"An assassin and thief and who knows what else for hire I've faced off with in the past," I said. "They call her the Chameleon and for some reason she lured me here to California. More than likely to set me up for just this purpose."

Dune spluttered while Miller's blue eyes watched

me carefully.

"You think this Chameleon is trying to frame you for murder," he said. "Why would she do that?"

"Because every time we encounter one another I kick her butt." Not accurate, but whatever. They weren't there and I was and I came out on top every time, thank you. Mostly. Kinda. Forget it, okay? Moving on. "She's pissed at me and wanted revenge. Or, more likely, is using me somehow to get what she really wants."

"Which is?" Miller was most definitely the smarter cookie.

"There's a rumor," I said. "I'm sure you've both heard it by now. About Mom's jewelry, diamonds from some Saudi prince. They went missing the day she died, and everyone thinks she hid them in Lucille."

"Did she?" Miller's interest had my back up.

"Why, do you want them for yourself, detective?" That challenge was met with a grin.

"Heard they're worth a lot of *denaro*," he said.

I shrugged at that. "I guess. They were pretty, sparkly." Memories again, back to that moment Mom opened the box, the glittering jewels catching the light, her husband scowling, the prince leaning close. "My guess is, the Chameleon wanted me as a distraction so she could get her hands on the car and find the jewelry."

"A rather elaborate scheme," Miller said. "Why not just search it?"

"You don't think it hasn't been?" Okay, this was

over. "Think what you want, but I'll tell you what everyone who has ever asked me the total and honest truth. My mother didn't hide anything in Lucille except her ego and she didn't even hide that."

Both the agent and detective exchanged a look, Dune finally sighing and nodding as Miller went on.

"Ashe Yoshida," he said, Agent Dune backing off, letting him carry on while she listened. "She's a known associate of Roman Sebastian."

"So?" Great, don't tell me my sperm donor was about to cause me trouble too.

Elle's soft hiss spoke much louder than Miller's casual reply.

"No biggie," he said. "He's just an international criminal INTERPOL has never been able to pin anything on despite decades of illegal activity across four continents."

Simone jumped in on that. "Which has nothing to do with Petal," she said. "Aside from the fact you *allege* such things since if INTERPOL really knew for certain this Roman Sebastian was a criminal they'd have managed to put together a case against him by now."

Miller shrugged.

While Dune spoke up.

"Why did you meet with Roman Sebastian, Ms. Morgan?"

And now it was out there in the open and, instead of answering, on impulse, wanting to shield because I hadn't had time to warn him where I went, I spun on Dad with an appeal on my face. To trust me, to not jump to conclusions. While his own filled with grief and then hardened when he looked away.

"What does Roman Sebastian have to do with any of this?" Dad confronted Agent Dune while my heart broke. He knew. Of course he knew. Had to have guessed.

She went on, oblivious to the damage she'd done to my real father and to hell with Roman Sebastian. "Ashe Yoshida was present at the auction," she said. "We suspect Mr. Sebastian was attempting to purchase the car."

"You suspect," Simone said. "I see. And the fact you suspect someone you've called an international criminal wanted an item the dead man possessed, instead of questioning him about the murder you instead, what? Choose to pursue Petal for going for a run in the middle of the night because she can't sleep out of grief and the loss of her childhood." Oh, she was *good*. Like, epically good. I wouldn't have wanted to be on the stand if she was going to question me because I would cave so fast.

The FBI agent seemed to find that a frustration but the detective never shifted from that mild amusement lingering on his face.

"For your information," I said because it was going to come out and I didn't want to hold anything back and give them reason to question me again, "I've only just discovered Roman Sebastian had an affair with my mother." I swallowed, the shaking that I'd fought off, the shock, finally emerging but only because I let it. Just enough for authenticity. "The man who killed Annette Morgan, the man I'd thought was my biological father," I'm so sorry, Dad, "turns out he wasn't."

Miller caught on first, whistled low, while Agent Dune took a moment to catch up. When she did, triumph crossed her face a moment, though what she thought she'd just won I had no idea.

"Roman's your daddy, huh?" Miller shook his head. "That's tough, kid."

"Enough." Simone put herself firmly between us, gesturing for the detective to leave and, to my surprise, he did, joining the agent in the hallway. My lawyer friend stood firm, hand on the door. "Go find some real evidence or leave my client alone. And I'm not kidding. I'll have your butts in court so fast for harassment you'll both be out of jobs before you can catch your breath." And, with that, she slammed the heavy door shut before turning on me with her red face twisting in anger. "What," she snarled, "was *that*?"

Remember how I mentioned I'd lost the ability to care about what happened to me? I shrugged, and that went over well. If steam could have come out her ears, it would have.

But Elle interrupted her before she could shout at me. "I need to talk to Miller." And exited. Dad followed her so fast I missed catching his hand, though I tried, I swear I did. He glanced back before closing the door on me and I let him go. Only because his expression begged me to. While Simone carried on her angry tirade, not a word getting through to me. I wasn't here with her at the moment. I was out there, with my dad.

We'd talk later. I hoped."

CHAPTER ELEVEN

B Y THE TIME I'D paced a hole in the carpet (exaggerating, but still), the sun had set and I was ready to climb out of my skin and scream over being trapped in the room, not knowing what was going on.

"That's it," Reggie said, surging to her feet, grabbing her bag, draping it over her forearm as she slid into her shining black heels. How she looked so put-together after the afternoon and evening we'd had I really couldn't say because a glance in the mirror over the sofa told me I hadn't fared nearly as well. "Petal needs to blow off steam. Let's hit the bar."

Simone's instant protest died when I stopped in my tracks. "Great idea," I said to my bestie. "Let's get more gin into me so I can really make a fool of myself this time." Reggie faltered but I was already pocketing my returned wallet and slipping into my sandals, phone in hand, expectation on my face while the two women exchanged a look. "I meant it," I said. "I have deep and abiding need to be foolish and laugh a little and pretend I'm not a freaking train wreck. You two in, or am I doing this alone?"

Reggie flashed me those perfect white teeth and hooked her arm through mine, Simone following with some reluctance, though she did come with us, so at least I had one person who had my back who wanted to rein me in. Reggie? Would cheer me on. Which meant I had a balance of angel and devil to work with and that suited me just fine.

Thing was, I couldn't decide which was which and no way was I asking their opinion.

That's how we found ourselves at the hotel bar at 7PM, a gin already gone down far too easily while we ordered way too much food for three women, my stomach demanding I at least eat something before dumping more alcohol after the initial dose.

It was a surprise I found myself relaxing and actually laughing as I'd hoped and chatting with the two amazing women I was lucky enough to have in my life? Yeah, me too, and not about to question my luck, either. Whatever happened from here on in I was going to make sure I put myself in positions like this one much more than the uncomfortable and memory-inducing ones I'd stumbled into.

My second drink gone, I volunteered a trip to the bar, the single waitress clearly overworked and underpaid and not as friendly as the smiling bartender with his lovely brown eyes and flirtatious wink. Order placed, I leaned into the polished wooden surface between two stools, a familiar voice interrupting my humming attempt at happiness in the face of a murder investigation.

"Corinne, if there's anything I can do moving ahead," the man said, easily recognizable when I glanced his way. Paxton Hunter, right? The MC and owner of the auction event. And with him, none other than the woman I'd overheard on the phone at the bar, Edison Fisher's wife and now the owner of Lucille. "Please don't hesitate to ask."

"There is one thing." She leaned in to him, in a much more flirtatious than concerned manner than she likely realized. "I'm worried, Paxton. Yosef Moshe is challenging Lucille's provenance. He says there are irregularities in the authentication. But I know Edison had the original paperwork. He bought her shortly after Annette Morgan died, right from the property. He's had her in our possession ever since."

Grunt and a gut punch I really wasn't expecting. Not only was her husband dead, he was a vulture who'd been one of the pack of ravening animals who'd swarmed over Mom's estate and picked it clean. I couldn't help the twisting of my lips, the glare I fixed at the bar's top. Hey, I didn't glare at them, so don't give me a hard time.

The bartender returned with my order, but I couldn't bring myself to leave just yet, the conversation keeping me thralled and in place despite myself.

"Yosef just wants a closer look at the car," Paxton said, patting her arm, doing nothing to repel her advances as she brushed against his shoulder with her truly epic bosom. Bought and paid for, no doubt, by her dead husband, but who was I to judge?

Me. I was *me*. The daughter of the dead woman that same dead husband got Lucille from. Judgy-judgy judgepants, yup, all over the place, so sue me.

Corinne nodded. "I know," she said. "But if he can cast doubt on the provenance, I'm worried about my investment. What should I do?"

It was clear to me she really didn't care so much about the car or its relationship to my mother's death. She was just using it as an excuse to get close to the auction's host. Thing was, I'd had just enough gin to prod me into raining on her little parade of silicone and sorrow because vindictiveness, it turned out, was now a part of my makeup.

"Maybe I can help." I turned with a grim grin on my face, two drinks forgotten, my own in hand, catching movement out of my peripheral vision, two women hot-footing toward me while I closed the distance between myself and the now staring couple. "You want proof Lucille is authentic?"

The widow, now retreating from Paxton in surprise, nodded after glancing at him for confirmation. His focus and attention, however, wasn't so divided, his professional smile flashing into place as he stuck out his hand with that same gameshow host voice he'd used earlier returning.

"You must be Petal Morgan," he said. "Paxton

Hunter. What an honor, Ms. Morgan."

Yeah, yeah, stick it somewhere someone who cared could have raptures over it.

"Petal." Reggie reached me first, though Simone was right beside her, flanking me, the gorgeous black woman with her massive hair and authoritative stance no more impressive than the sternly commanding brunette with her pale, perfect skin and courtroom litigator confidence doing their best by sheer will alone to contain me.

Impossible, poor dears. I would not be contained.

"I asked you a question, Mrs. Fisher," I said, not bothering to jerk my arm free from Reggie's grasp, ignoring Simone's whispers of warning in my ear. I was much too far gone for either of them to reach me because how fun was this, the chance to make matters worse?

There would come a time, the next morning more than likely, I realized gin and I weren't friends and I needed to choose a new kind of alcohol when under investigation for murder. But tonight? Tonight was no time for thinking things through or regret. This was the time for action.

And I couldn't wait to start the show.

"Yes, of course." Corinne Fisher spluttered. "You're… are you really her?" Why did she sound so freaked out? Oh, right.

"I didn't kill your husband," I said. "But I can prove beyond a shadow of a doubt Lucille is who the paperwork says she is. If you're interested."

Corinne glanced at Paxton one more time—

couldn't she make up her mind for herself?—while I guzzled my drink (oh, yes I did, because more gin was the answer) and the auctioneer nodded to her.

"Why, yes, I'd love that." She swallowed hard, blushed deeply.

"I just bet you would." I emptied my glass, beamed a smile and marched past her, the girls trying to grab me but not succeeding, Reggie's hand slipping free when I tugged just hard enough I knew it would leave a bruise. Before I spun back to the staring foursome. "Well? What are you waiting for?"

I turned and marched on, not caring if they followed but hearing their footsteps behind me, Simone reaching me first this time.

"Petal, what are you doing?" She barely raised her voice above a whisper, but it got through.

"Helping the widow," I said.

"You're doing no such thing," she snapped as Reggie caught up with us.

"Petal, I love you, but you are one crazy-ass woman, you know that?" My bestie sounded as amused as she was exasperated. "You're going to get us all arrested."

"You're free to go back to your drinks," I said, carrying on. "I have something I need to do." Because I did, damn it. Simone was 100% right. This had nothing to do with helping Corinne Fisher authenticate Lucille.

This had everything to do with finally getting to say goodbye to my mother.

I noticed him watching as we approached the

entry to the event space, Yosef Moshe standing from the chair where he hunched over his phone, drifting closer while I stopped at last and nodded toward the cop guarding the entry.

"Reg," I said. "Think you can distract him?"

She sighed, tossed her curls while Simone groaned. "Watch me." Oh, I did, and so did the cop on duty once he saw her coming, all swinging hips and full lips and come hither stares. By the time she made it to his side he was grinning and, just a moment later, she had him lured away from his post to a more private side corridor where she met my eyes and nodded.

Time to get this party started.

The door wasn't locked so it was easy enough to slip through, Simone staying close, Paxton and Corinne behind her and, of course, Yosef Moshe joining the entourage. I ignored all the glass cases, heading at that same ground-eating stride toward the back of the room where the curtain had finally been drawn back, Lucille's front seat empty again, the car crouching there in her red and white splendor, watching me.

Waiting for me.

Yes, I was well aware anthropomorphizing the thing meant I likely had an incurable mental illness and maybe I was actually already in a straight jacket and padded room and this was all some delusion of my broken mind. Whatever the truth, this was my chance and I was taking it.

Wasn't lost on me this was the kind of stunt

Mom would have loved and approved of.

It wasn't until I reached Lucille and climbed the podium to stand next to her I caught my breath. Ran my fingertips over the driver's side door to the handle. I'd never been allowed to sit in the driver's seat. Still pristine despite the dead man who'd been sitting there just a few hours ago, his obviously bloodless end leaving not a trace of him behind on the red leather. Why then did it feel like decades of hurt still lurked here, the kind of filth that would never wash clean?

"Well?" That was Yosef, I recognized his accent. "Is it Lucille, Ms. Morgan?"

I looked up, realized we'd added two more. Ashe Yoshida, to my surprise (though I shouldn't have been, I suppose) stood next to Yosef and, lurking behind them, the tall and awkward Marlon Landon. Oh look, the gang's all here, though we were missing Reggie, of course, and Agent Dune, Detective Miller. Elle. Oh, and my dad.

And my other dad. Maybe the fact Ashe was here meant Roman didn't count anyway.

"It's Lucille," Marlon spoke up, though he shrunk physically when Yosef turned to glare at him. "Leave Ms. Morgan alone."

I waved off the attempt at chivalry, memory cutting them off anyway as I looked down into the car and was suddenly

—*driving down the winding ocean-side highway with the sun bright overhead and Mom in the front seat, the scent of her lost in the smell of the water, her long, blue silk scarf trailing behind her, hat fluttering in the wind, the sound of her laughter so amazing to me I could barely stand it.*

"Petal," she said, looking down at where I sat in the passenger's seat, my feet not touching the floor, the hem of my dress flapping, hands clutching the seatbelt across my chest as she drove too fast, wove into the other lane then back again with that same careless laughter. "This is all that matters in life, Petal. Money and power and my most favorite thing in the whole world." I knew I was smiling in return, I couldn't help myself. When she was like this, everything was forgiven and all right again and I loved her so much it hurt. Until she threw her arms in the air. "I love you, Lucille!" And laughed.

In my face.

While my fragile and hopeful little heart.

Broke—

I know I must have looked like a headcase, because it was the jerking flinch of my entire body that shook me out of the memory.

Like I cared what I looked like.

"Hello, Lucille," I whispered.

CHAPTER TWELVE

I DIDN'T CLIMB IN the driver's side. Not out of any old edict from my mother, because wherever she was burning, she could bite me.

No, I used the passenger's side because that was where my proof lay. My slow walk felt like circling a threatening predator as if the moment I stood in front of her bumper and the four round headlights stared me down, that gaping grill like an open mouth laughing at me, the car would roar to life of her own and run me down for daring to defile her.

Didn't happen. The wakening of Lucille, I mean. The defiling, on the other hand?

My proof came at a price to the classic car's interior. Something a vindictive little girl carved into the underside of the dash with a very sharp penknife she stole from her mother's chauffeur.

My hand sought it, rather than my sight, because

I wasn't eight anymore and tucking myself under the dash in the two-seater would be impossible. Didn't mean I couldn't find what I was looking for and did, memory guiding my fingertips until they traced over the indentations.

It was my phone's turn to do the job. I angled it so I could see, using the flash to illuminate what I was looking for and snapped a picture before sitting back to stare at it a second.

"Mrs. Fisher," I called out at last, gaze still locked on *Petal Morgan was here* inside a crooked heart making my eyes burn, my throat tighten. The rather blasé and cliched statement had so much more meaning than just what it read, my need to exist, to be noticed, after a life of neglect, all so perfectly contained inside those four simple words, that off center representation of the agony I felt every day, all day.

Until the night she died.

Corinne joined me with some reluctance, taking the phone and looking at the image before I slid sideways up against the center console and guided her hand to the carving. She stared at me in mute horror, though whether at the desecration of a classic like Lucille or because she understood my hurt I didn't know and didn't really give a crap. But when she backed away, she was a believer.

They took turns as I called them up, though before Paxton could take his go at voyeurism, Ashe stepped in, forcing him to back down. She didn't comment, none of them did, Yosef's grunt of acknowledgment and squinting glance at me only making me angry.

"I told you," Marlon said, not bothering to take his turn, hanging back. "I told you this was Lucille."

"Which leaves only one question, Ms. Morgan," Yosef said. "Where is the missing jewelry?"

They watched with eager anticipation, all of them. Even Simone seemed caught up in the moment, as though I had some big reveal for them all.

Well, I hated to disappoint. "For pity's sake," I said, sighing. "You're all deluded if you think my mother would do anything with any kind of foresight, let alone actually prevent people from seeing the diamonds. The exact opposite. Her vanity wouldn't have let her do anything of the sort. So please, take my word for it. Mom didn't hide anything valuable in Lucille."

Tell that to the LAPD, Petal. Oh, and the very angry FBI agent who stormed in with a smirking detective on her heels, Reggie in cuffs—what?—and the bigger mess I'd just made no longer seeming like such a good idea.

"Downtown, Ms. Morgan," Agent Dune snarled. "Now."

Except, I didn't get to follow that order, not right away. Because Elle and Dad had perfect timing, and before Dune could wrangle any of us under control, they took over.

"Celia," my father said in that tone of voice no one ever managed to stand against that I'd ever witnessed. She was no exception either, backing down before she realized she'd done so, the automatic reaction turning to anger as she scowled at falling into line so easily.

"This isn't your case, Andy." She tried to step between him and Lucille, and me, if I was going to be fair, but Dad either didn't care or didn't notice or both because he kept coming and she was finally forced to get out of the way before he strode his big and overbearing way through her.

"Petal," Dad said, hand held up toward me when he stopped at the foot of the pedestal. "It's time to go."

"Don't you want to see?" I waved for him to join me, nodded to Dune, too. "What Petal Morgan did to her mother's precious car?"

Dad glanced at the photo but didn't bother to take me up on my offer to show him where I'd left my mark, though Dune did, and, to my surprise, Miller. Elle held back, hands in her pockets, standing very close to Reggie who didn't seem so much angry as she was annoyed by her present circumstance.

"Can we please uncuff my friend?" I met Dune's eyes. "She didn't do anything."

"She interfered with an investigation," Dune said.

"She flirted with a cop who shouldn't have left his post," I said. "You arrested the wrong person." The officer in question flinched, coughed softly into one hand, while Miller laughed and crossed to Reggie, divesting her of the bracelets.

"Nice play," he said to my friend.

She batted her lashes. "Just being friendly, detective."

Again he laughed, shaking his head, before looking up at me. "So you broke in here to say goodbye to your mother's car and to reminisce over vandalism, is that it, Ms. Morgan."

"You got it," I said, climbing out of Lucille and purposely slamming the heavy door while Corinne Fisher winced. "There was question about provenance." I met Yosef's eyes. "I take it that question has been put to rest?"

He nodded after a moment, shrugged. "I accept the item's authenticity," he said.

"Good for you." I stepped down off the podium, forcing Dune to follow me instead of the other way around, Dad pausing, I noticed when I turned to look up, one hand on Lucille's passenger door before he sighed and descended.

I wasn't the only one with memories, but his had a lot of blood after the fact while mine hadn't left outside scars.

Just gaping holes inside.

"You might think this is acceptable," Dune returned to her attempt at seizing control so predictably I almost grinned (thanks, gin), "but regardless the needs of the owner, this is still a crime scene."

"Tell me about it," I said. I knew I was being mouthy and couldn't blame the alcohol completely. That causality I placed solely on my mother and how she raised me. "Everything connected to Annette Morgan ended in a crime scene." I backed away when Dune reached for me, seeing her anger in her eyes, knowing she was about to accuse me of resisting arrest. "I'm sorry Edison Fisher got caught up in my mother's curse," I said. "I'm sorry the man died in her ugly ass car," I flipped a very rude gesture at Lucille who had the decency not to argue, "and I'm sorry you're so short-freaking-sighted you think I had anything to do with his murder to the point you're likely letting the real killer walk." Oh, I was on a roll and they'd have to gag me to shut me up, still backing away, Simone's death-glare almost worse than Dad's hurt expression. "I'm sorry I listened to the Chameleon and I'm sorry my biological father is an international criminal. I'm sorry I have a sister I've never met and just found out about and that my daddy couldn't keep it in his pants. But most of all, I'm sorry you found me, Dad." Hey, where had these tears come from? I was crying all of a sudden and I certainly didn't give permission for the waterworks to start up because that wasn't on the agenda. Except, apparently, it was. I hiccupped a sob before going on. "I'm sorry he didn't kill me, too, and I'm sorry I'm such a screwup." I turned, rage driving me, and grabbed a plastic glass on one of the display cases, someone's discarded drink. Heaved it at Lucille. It didn't make it, but the liquid inside did, splashing over her whitewalls with a splattering of red wine that made Corinne Fisher cry out. "I hate that car," I yelled. "I hated my mother and I just wanted to make this end. Finally end." I felt my knees crumple, held onto the case next to me but I needn't have bothered because Dad was there, arms around me and I was eight again and hugging him while he soothed me with soft words and shielded my eyes from seeing what was left of my mother while I buried my face in his chest and wept.

For the poor sad and pathetic victim, Petal Morgan. Boo hoo.

CHAPTER THIRTEEN

D ID YOU THINK MY little outburst meant Dune cut me slack and patted my head and sent me home? Understood completely my emotional state and took it for the truth? Or my word for it I didn't kill anyone and was being set up by a criminal who was either after my mother's long-lost jewels and thought framing me for kicks was a good side gig or had lost her freaking mind and was now on my hit-list?

Um. About that.

Funny how you've seen one interrogation room, you've seen them all.

The last time I'd been here I had a headache from too much afternoon gin and being accused of murder. This time was *so* much better (insert unnecessarily angsty sarcasm here). Not only had my previous calamity evolved from a dull throb into a migraine that had me resting my forehead on the cold metal table because it felt so good just to sit there and let the chill soothe me despite knowing how bad it looked, I now had handcuffs uncomfortably holding me to the table wrenching my shoulders at awkward angles I ignored because that discomfort didn't hold a candle to the benefits of previously mentioned forehead and table connection.

The cuffs really were overkill as far as I was concerned, though I did recall jerking free of the hand that tore me away from Dad, spinning on Dune with a snarl, only to find myself pinned to the wall with everyone shouting (including me, I think, some bad, bad words mingling with hysterical laughter) before being roughly restrained and shoved rather unceremoniously into the hall, the elevator, trapped with the detective and furious agent, my loved ones barred from entry, only to find myself firmly placed into the back seat of a cruiser and taken to a different building than the precinct I'd previously visited.

FBI office, hard to miss with the giant logo disk in the lobby and all those suits pausing to stare, the metal detector that loved my cuffs and the belt buckle I wore, all the way to a new elevator and musak and the still raging Dune who didn't say a freaking word to me the whole time, face a mask of that anger I knew she barely contained (not very FBI of her, all together too emotional for someone in her position) until I was dropped off in this present position of small room, camera, one-way mirror, table, forehead, cuffs.

Groan.

I had no idea up to this point how long I'd sat with my head down and my heart beating a little too fast and the desire to curl into the fetal position making me nauseated every time I tried to sit up. The banging in my skull matched the *da-dum* of my pulse, something to focus on instead of the epic screwup I'd just unfolded on myself. Come on, though, Dune was clearly having a bad day and taking it out on me to treat me this way.

I had enough guilt to relive in sequence over and over again maybe I thought I deserved it.

You know when you're so wrapped up in an overly convoluted emotional state you can't sort out what's grief and what's anger and what's fear and all you can do is let it take you on the ride it has in mind while you wish you were dead?

No? Just me, huh? Okies.

I swallowed hard, realizing my mouth hung open as I breathed through it, panting just a little, the pain in my head taking all my energy. The sound of the door opening reminded me I needed to find a way to focus and defend myself, but I just couldn't muster the energy to sit up. Not until I heard a soft voice I knew, felt her touch on my shoulder.

"Petal," Simone said, sitting next to me, the sight of her bare knees and high heels and the hem of her black skirt so much lawyer mode compared to the jeans she'd been wearing I managed to push myself back and meet her eyes, though I had to squint through the ache the light overhead increased, illumination piercing my gaze and diving directly into my brain. She handed me a pair of pills, setting an open bottle of water next to me, bless her. I took the meds, awkwardly with the cuffs in place, three tries before my hands stopped fighting the restraints, fingers making it to my mouth. I dribbled out of the corner of my lips when I tried to drink, refusing Simone's offer of help. Stubborn, I wiped at the lost moisture with the shoulder of my shirt, managing a nod of thanks, before nudging the bottle aside and letting my head hang.

"Petal." Oh, she wasn't done. "I need you to listen to me, please." I met her gaze out of the corner of my eye. "You have to let me talk for you. No more oversharing." While her anger was gone, she wasn't messing around, I could tell. There was enough worry in her I nodded again, sniffing, lifting my head, coming back to reality. Though it was far too early for the pills to have kicked in, I felt the pain recede and knew the agony was on me. All me. Lovely. "Petal, do you understand?"

I didn't get to speak, clearing my throat to try, when the door opened again and Agent Dune entered. She didn't look at either one of us, a large document box in her hands, MORGAN, PETAL written across the front in thick, black marker. Which made me chuckle because I grew up with an FBI agent for a dad. I knew what that box was. A prop, meant to make me fear her.

I was so far from afraid of Celia Dune she had no idea. The demons that plagued me? Way scarier than she could ever be.

"We've collected a lot of evidence against you, Ms. Morgan." Dune's crisp confidence had me grinning, something that clearly infuriated her all over again. "It's a shame you're not taking this seriously. You're going to go to prison for a very long time for what you've done. The other inmates won't find you so amusing."

"If you had proof," Simone spoke while I did as she wanted and held my tongue if not the curve of my mouth, "she'd be under formal arrest. Not this," my friend and lawyer waved at the cuffs pinning my hands to the table, "unwarranted treatment you can be assured will lead to misconduct charges, Agent Dune."

"We'll see," Dune snapped back. "Well, Ms. Morgan? Are you ready to drop the poor me act and confess? Or do I have to send you to lockup while we finish preparing your case?"

"That will never happen," Simone said, cold, icy cold. "Stop trying to intimidate my client with your ridiculous bullying tactics, agent. It's really beneath someone like you."

The door opened before Dune could argue further, Detective Peter Miller poking his nose in. He gestured for Dune to join him, but she shook her head, scowling while he shrugged and grinned at me, crossing with his keys in his hands, uncuffing me while Dune spluttered and he spoke.

"Turns out we found a witness, one of the hotel staff, who saw you in the gym, Ms. Morgan." He stepped back when I was free, that automatic reaction to rub my wrists now that the restraints were gone so classic I grinned back. Surreal, that's what this was. One big mistake wrapped in a cloud of what the actual and smothered in a sense of detachment from reality. Any second now some guy with a clapboard was going to show up and yell, "Cut!"

Didn't happen but would have been cool.

Dune's teeth grinding was audible, her fury now aimed at the LAPD detective. "Is this so-called witness reliable?"

"The hotel's night manager," Miller said. "Checked in on her three times, he said. Saw her go in, mid-run and just before she finished. Said he remembered her because he'd never seen anyone run so fast." He met my eyes. "What *are* you running from, Ms. Morgan?"

I flashed him my teeth. "Am I free to go?" I'd broken Simone's no talking rule, but she didn't seem to mind, instantly getting to her feet and pulling me up next to her.

"You are," she said before either could confirm. "And, as I said, I'll be speaking to your superiors about your treatment of my client. Believe me when I say you've stepped deep into something you should have walked away from. Good evening to you both."

CHAPTER FOURTEEN

A ND JUST LIKE THAT, I was out in the hallway of the FBI office, following Simone to the entry, only to have Dune emerge behind me.

"Ms. Morgan," she called out. "Stay away from my crime scene or I will arrest you for interfering with the investigation. Are we clear?"

She just had to have the last word. Which meant I ignored her, naturally.

It wasn't until we were on the street, the humidity of the California evening unrelenting, that I realized Detective Miller followed us, Elle shaking his hand where she waited next to the SUV they must have rented, Dad standing next to her, Reggie rushing forward to hug me and Simone.

"Thanks for the tip," the rumpled detective said.

Elle shrugged. "Not the first time I did your job

for you, Miller."

He chuckled. "I seem to recall you pulled my but out of a few scrapes, Gordon, but I always paid my debts." Miller waved at me. "Stay out of trouble, okay? I'm tired of dealing with the feds and Dune in particular." He grinned at Dad. "No offense, Agent Walker, but you Bureau types can be a pain in the patootie."

Dad nodded. "I'm aware," he said. "Thank you for following up, Detective Miller."

"I never liked you for it," Miller said to me directly. "Just didn't make sense. But Dune's a dog with a bone and she seems to have some kind of grudge." He squinted at Dad. "Anything to do with you, Agent Walker?"

Dad didn't answer. I thought back to my first (well, second, if she was telling the truth) time I met Celia Dune. She hadn't seemed antagonistic, though my drunken state meant I'd been unable to read her completely. Hadn't there been some emotion that she'd struggled with I couldn't identify at the time? Whatever her problem was, she could kiss my behind.

I was out of here. Except, the moment Dad turned to me, gesturing at the car, I resisted.

"We're leaving for DC immediately," he said at his most demanding special agent.

"Who's the new prime suspect?" Dune told me to stay out of her investigation, but if this was the Chameleon's doing, that meant she was here in LA. As much as I wanted to go home and forget all about this, I had a chance to catch her if I played my cards right. This wasn't about Mom or closure any longer. This was about my nemesis and me and I was suddenly so furiously overwhelmed with the need to choke the living crap out of her I was trembling.

Miller answered while Dad just glared at me. "We don't have anything solid," he said. "Looking at the wife, but she has a weak alibi I doubt will stand up for TOD. Doesn't mean she didn't hire someone." Someone I knew and despised so much at the moment I would have shot her in the face given the chance and not thought twice about it? "We're also looking into the Israeli buyer, Yosef Moshe."

"And Ashe Yoshida," I said, not looking away from the tight and angry expression in Dad's eyes. "Roman Sebastian's lackey."

"All three were seen on camera near the event around TOD," he said. "The fact Paxton Hunter didn't think to check the car after the setup was complete has me a little curious about him, but he has a solid alibi himself."

"Petal," Dad said. "Let's go home."

Simone touched my arm, Reggie's dark eyes full of sadness. But it was Elle Gordon who shook Miller's hand, then crossed to the SUV, pulled open the back door. Turned to me with her gray eyes flat and expressionless, who won me over.

"Get your ass in the truck," she said in a soft and pleasant voice. "We're done here."

I cracked a smile. Couldn't help myself. Hugged her on the way by. Did as I was told, huddling in the back seat with Reggie beside me, Simone on her left, Dad driving while Elle took the passenger's side, one of her hands reaching back to squeeze my knee though she didn't say another word.

She didn't have to. They were right, all of them, and hadn't my first instinct been to go home and forget I even thought this might be a good idea? I had to get out of LA. It was having a horrible influence on me.

So why then when we returned to the hotel, well past midnight, did I find myself sitting on the edge of the bed, staring at the floor with my hands clenched in my lap? I'd only taken a shower because Reggie made me, but couldn't bring myself to lie down because every time I did, every time I closed my eyes, memory took me over.

Lovely. Another sleepless night. No wonder I was a mess. Oh, wait. That happened first, right. No excuses, then.

I could have packed. The jet had left to retrieve agents for another case, so we were stuck waiting for a commercial flight the next morning. I had lots of time to sit and ponder and relive and hurt. Forced myself into a prone position, breathed deep, closed my eyes.

—crouched in her clothes I'd pulled down around me, heard her screams, his grunts, the sound of the blows—

And then, something new.

—peeked out into the room—

Wait, what? Oh my god. So it *was* true. It had to be, not a false memory at all. Why had I forgotten

107

until now? One look, I'd taken one look. A look I'd forgotten I'd sneaked, the memory long suppressed, smothered in denial and the need to protect my mind, but it was there, bubbling to the surface.

—one look, enough to see her, see him, see the open bedroom door, and a face—

I sat up abruptly, heart pounding so hard I was positive a heart attack was imminent, grasping at my chest with both hands, crying silently, rocking myself.

Someone was there? Someone watched my mother's husband beat her to death and didn't do a thing to stop him. Or help me.

Who was it?

I leaped out of bed, my pulse slowing enough the dizziness of my elevated blood pressure didn't send me into an immediate floor puddle but it was a close call. Instead, I paced, fast and hard, across the room and back again, mind scouring for the truth though I shied from it still, finally stopping my endless back and forth and closing my eyes with my teeth grinding together.

Made myself look.

Petal. *Look.*

A face. There was a face. I had shielded myself from the memory, all this time. Wrapped that instant of horror in whatever protections my eight-year-old's mind had at her disposal, shoved it down so deep it only found its way up to conscious thought now. And while I was aware that memories couldn't always be trusted, I trusted this one.

Knew in my gut I'd not just heard her die, but

seen it. Seen her husband shoot himself and collapse on top of her.

And I wasn't the only one.

Who that face belonged to I had no idea. The recollection was too muddy, the pale face too fragmented through the partially open door. Backed by the hall's light, indistinct to my little girl's memory. But it was there, of that I was positive.

There had been another witness.

The burning need to know who it was hit me with such irrational anger I had to hug myself tight to keep from flying apart. It took a long few minutes of deep breathing and choking on tears and wrestling my demons to finally regain control.

And, oddly enough, the thing that ultimately helped me calm down and relax? Lucille. My burdened and aching mind flickered away from that night, the new memory, the truth that someone let her die and didn't do anything about it, didn't try to save me, morphed into a thought.

A thought I grasped onto with the aching need of a drowning person reaching for buoyancy. Had me throwing on clothes and sneakers and stuffing my hair under a ballcap, slipping out into the living room, Reggie's door closed, my bestie hopefully asleep. And sneaking like a thief out into the hall and to the stairs—no elevator, I needed the run down to the main floor to burn off some of the anxious jitters—until I was jogging across the lobby and outside into the California night.

Fresh air. A walk. Escape from the confines of

my body if not my mind. I know what you're thinking. Who in their right mind goes for a stroll in LA at one in the morning? Crazy people, that's who. Folks with a death wish or something illegal to sell or a broken woman who really needed meds.

I didn't walk far. In fact, I made it about a block before I stopped short, distracted, attention taken and gratefully, despite Celia Dune and her last command. Maybe because of it? Probably because of it. She could suck it.

Whatever my ultimate reasoning, it had me circling the building to the lot behind the hotel, stopping at the access to the convention area and auction site for staff and loading/unloading.

I stared at the elevated sliding garage doors for a moment, the set of steps to the narrow black steel doorway. Noted the cameras over the bays, scowled at the emptiness of the parking lot, the scent of hot asphalt lingering along with composting waste from the hotel's dumpsters.

The door opened even as I contemplated, a young man in a black apron over his matching shirt and pants emerging, the headscarf he wore tied tightly over his dark curls. He seemed surprised to find me there, but didn't pause until he was at the bottom of the stairs, an unlit cigarette dangling from between his lips.

I approached as his silver lighter snapped into life, the glowing ember firing up as he inhaled. He offered me a smoke, but I waved it off, hoping I didn't look like a crazy person as I smiled and did my best to be friendly while panicked hysteria battled for control over this stupid errand I used to try to shove it back down where it belonged.

"Hey, you work here?" Oh, Petal, you could do better than that.

He just shrugged, flicked the ash from his cigarette.

"Where does that door go?" I pointed at the exit he'd used, internally wincing because I wasn't up to this and despite what I knew was a weak and trembling smile, no way was he going to help me.

"Back entry to the kitchens," he said. "And the convention center."

His willingness to talk helped me relax a little, though I was no less bumbling in my questioning, apparently, because I pointed up at the cameras. "These working, do you know?" I needed to stop talking and go back to bed and try to forget. "I'm looking into the murder." Weak, kid. Really weak.

His gaze followed mine, another long drag following. "Nope," he said. "Like I told the other cop, they've been out for almost a week." He stepped on the butt he dropped to the ground. "You're with her right? The hot blonde cougar in the cowboy boots."

Elle, though if she'd heard his description she'd likely have cuffed him and sent him downtown just for spite. Part of the reason I loved her. Instead of defending her honor, however (forgive me, Elle), I nodded immediately. "Yes, exactly," I said. "So, no footage of last night." Which meant this was the perfect entry if someone wanted to get into the hall and kill Edison Fisher. Something Agent Celia Dune failed to mention.

And the Chameleon's plan suddenly made perfect sense.

CHAPTER FIFTEEN

THE CHEF LEFT ME there after a minute, going back inside while I continued to stare at the black painted door with my nemesis on my mind.

No wonder she set me up as the murderer. It was to hide the fact she was the killer. She could easily have lured Edison Fisher to meet her in the convention hall under the lie she was me, murdered him and slipped out again. And while we didn't have that kind of relationship where she wanted me in prison, I hadn't thought, if she'd been hired to kill him and had a point to prove against me, I wouldn't put it past her to frame me just for kicks.

It had to have been a hire job. Someone had it in for Edison Fisher. Because if the Chameleon was after my mother's jewelry there would have been no reason to text the now-deceased owner. She could have just slipped inside and done a search of Lucille and no one would have been the wiser. No, his death had a point and someone was behind that point. One step behind, though, if they hired an assassin to do the deed for them.

So the question was, who wanted him dead and why? Dune was looking at this the wrong way because she was looking at me.

Now even more irritated than ever, I fired off a message of my own to the burner phone I'd left listed as unknown number in my contacts. *Thanks for the murder rap*, I sent, thumbs mashing the keys. *I knew you were an asshat, but I didn't know you were this resentful. Next time you decide to frame me, or contact me, or send me something uninvited, don't.*

Growl.

My next text was to Celia Dune, though I hesitated as I read over what I'd written. *You need to look into who wanted Edison Fisher dead. Because I didn't.* A terrible idea to send that off in the wee hours on no sleep and a lingering headache, right?

The phone vibrated in my hand before I could hit send. *I would never do something like that. You're now 0-2 in the accusation department.*

I snarled at the screen. *Forgive me if I don't believe a thief, murderer and liar. You convinced Edison Fisher you were me.*

You have the wrong person, she sent. *I had no idea anyone wanted him dead or I wouldn't have sent you to California in the first place.*

Again, like I believe you, I sent.

There was a pause while I stood there in the semi-darkness and shook, my rage making my knees tremble and my stomach clench.

Did you meet Daddy yet?

She did *not. Mind your own damned business.*

Then stop bringing me into it, she sent back. *Oh, and by the way, it* is *my business this time, Petal dearest.*

What did she mean by that? Those knots in my stomach tightened further as a horrible, wretched and truly unthinkable fear woke, rose to the surface, bubbled and asked for the chance to live. While I smothered all of it in denial so deep and so *hell to the no way* I had instant heartburn.

Cat got your tongue, little sister?

She. No. She didn't. She couldn't—

We have to watch out for one another.

I turned my phone off. Held the power button down long after the screen went dark. Stared at it a long, long time. While Roman Sebastian's face swam in my mind and his deep voice told me about my—

Oh. My. God.

I didn't even realize I was moving until I stumbled up the steps to the black door at the back of the building. Doing something was preferable to melting down over a truth I refused to accept. Instead, I could focus on taking action, even if that action got me arrested again, thrown into an interrogation room for the rest of my life.

If it wasn't her (I couldn't bring myself to name her and she would forever remain nameless in my head and I'd never, ever let her in again), someone had used my name to get Edison Fisher into the convention center at midnight the night he died. If I could sneak into that same space without anyone seeing me, I could prove it was someone else because I had an alibi.

Dumb. Yeah. I know. I tended to the dumb when faced with knowledge of the unacceptable variety. Bad habit, got it from Mom. So, it was either let myself break down over what I'd just discovered or do a dumb.

You already knew where this was going, so you're just as culpable.

I expected to at least encounter some kind of resistance, a cop, a security guard, some staff. Nope, nada. It was so easy to wander through the back hall of the rear of the hotel and to the entry to the convention center, to pass through the employee's door and into the silent space beyond I actually shook my head at the ridiculousness of it all. No locks, no alarms and no cameras. Management should have been ashamed of themselves.

It took me a moment of frustrated recrimination before I realized I wasn't the only person who'd figured out just how simple it was to break in. The thing was, he didn't notice I'd joined him, so it was just as easy to meander up to the podium and cross my arms over my chest, watching with a frown on my face as Yosef Moshe, entire body lying across the seats, lifted the carpet on the passenger's side.

"Looking for something?"

If our creeping around hadn't alerted anyone to

our presence, surely his shout of surprise did. Yosef sat up suddenly, eyes huge, until he realized who it was had caught him.

"The diamonds," he said. "Where are they?"

They were all deaf and as dumb as I was. "For the last freaking time," I said. "Mom didn't hide anything in Lucille."

My turn to jump and meep in surprise, the sound of a revolver's hammer cocking over my shoulder spinning me around. To face off with Corinne Fisher, her shining .38's muzzle in my face.

"Tell us now," she snarled, "or I'll kill you."

CHAPTER SIXTEEN

MAYBE IT WAS MY state of mind or perhaps more so the fact I'd been held at gunpoint in the past and was so over being threatened over something that never happened I didn't resist the snort of derision that escaped me when I hit her with a flat and disdainful gaze.

"Oh, put that away," I said. "It's not going to change the facts, Corinne, as much as you'd like it to. I can't create diamonds out of thin air." The longer I talked, the more panicked her face became, made worse when I turned away and ignored her, though keeping her in my periphery enough I saw the fish lipping, the anxious back and forth from me to Yosef, while I went on, jabbing a finger at Lucille. "It's a car, you guys. A '62 Corvette convertible. Its value comes from its own rarity and the fact the woman who gave birth to me decided she wanted it and convinced the producers to give it to her when the movie wrapped. That's it. My mother's butt cheeks and hand prints are the sum total of the added value so like it or lump it, but just freaking accept it already."

Yosef seemed to, sliding out of the car, approaching me with his expression dark, face a twisted frown. "I have it on excellent authority those diamonds were never returned to the original owner," he said. "Annette had to have done something with them."

"Your Saudi prince friend should have known better than to trust my mother with anything of value," I shot back, "including his heart if he gave her that, too. The truth is, Mom lost them. They went missing from the house. How do I know? Because she planned to wear them the night of the party." *The* party. "The night she died." Oh, how she'd screamed in rage, thrown things, broken her possessions in a fit of angst that had the maids running for their lives and me hiding in her closet, my favorite place to escape her volatility. I'd seen her angry and I'd seen her happy, but I'd never seen her enraged like that before. "The diamonds are gone." I tossed my hands, done trying to explain while I turned back to Corinne. She still pointed the gun in my general direction but the clear disappointment and rather acute anxiety on her face held the suggestion of guilt I couldn't resist. "You had more reason to kill him than I did," I said, knowing I shifted topics rather rapidly, catching her swift blinking before denial crossed her face. "Didn't you?"

She licked her lips, Yosef descending to join her though he made no move to take the gun.

"I don't know what you're talking about," Corinne said, the favorite lie of the culpable.

"Sure you do," I said. "What, did he cut you out of the sale or something? Or cut you off completely?" Ah, that was it, then. "Divorce pending you failed to tell the police about, Corinne?"

She snarled at me, but there were tears in her eyes, desperate tears. "You have no idea," she said.

"You'd be surprised." I sighed, tired at last, rubbing my face with both hands, adjusting the brim of my ballcap to try to ease the lingering headache. "People like him, they put money and power and cars and jewelry ahead of everyone and everything in their lives." She flinched, nodded. Caught herself as if only then realizing she'd agreed. "He was going to keep everything and give you nothing, so you killed him." I met Yosef's eyes. "And you helped, right?"

She didn't answer, but the Israeli did. "We had nothing to do with his death." He gently took the gun from Corinne, the last of her resistance gone before she hugged him tightly and wept on his shoulder. "We only meant to acquire the car and retrieve the jewelry. Edison never believed they were hidden in Lucille, but so many rumors abounded." He hugged Corinne with one arm. "I never intended to fall in love with you, my dear. But I would move Heaven to give you what you need." He met my eyes again, his dark ones full of anger. "I swear, that's all.

It was to be Corinne's victory over her atrocious husband. To find the jewels and prove to him what a fool he'd been."

"You were going to buy the car for her," I said. "But Ashe undercut you."

He nodded. "She made arrangements with Edison prior to the auction. We only found out after his death."

Which meant Ashe had no reason to kill him, either, not if Roman was getting what he wanted. But what if Edison had backed out or upped his price? No, the price thing didn't fit. A man like Roman Sebastian wouldn't have balked at more money. It had to have been the first idea, that Edison changed his mind. But what would make him? Or, if he hadn't, if someone found out about the presale? That made me think of Paxton Hunter. After all, it wouldn't look good for his business if people cut out his process or his profits. Then again, for all I knew, this kind of back-room dealing went on all the time. I was sure as long as the auction's owner got his cut, he'd look the other way.

Who did that leave me with? The Chameleon. Another buyer.

Wait, *me*? This wasn't my case and I really needed to go back to my room and get some sleep before Dune caught me again.

"We were here that night," Corinne said, muffled at first before she leaned away from Yosef. "The night Edison was killed." Interesting. Her boyfriend nodded to her as she pulled herself together, using the pocket square from his jacket to clean herself up. "I wanted a chance to search the car."

"You had it in your possession for years," I said. "Why not do it then?"

She shook her head, fury flashing. "Edison kept her locked up," she said. "In a glass case in his garage. Pressure plates and lasers and other ridiculous measures. He did so with all his cars, all his prizes." Wow, talk about paranoid. "This was the first time I had a chance to actually search the car since he bought it."

"You mean, since you heard the rumor about the diamonds," I said.

She shrugged at that. "We were about to approach the car that night when I heard someone coming so we ran." Corinne looked up at Yosef. "I didn't see anyone, but I assumed it was security or Paxton."

Her boyfriend nodded. "Neither of us saw who entered," he said. "It was almost midnight so I can only assume now it was Edison himself or perhaps even his murderer we heard."

I glared pointedly at the gun. "You know, that's not helping your case any. You both look guilty as sin."

"Agreed." Ashe stepped out of shadow and into the light, joining me, her own gun held level and steady at her hip. "And since this item now belongs to my employer, neither of you have the right any longer to search for anything."

"I told Roman I wasn't selling," Corinne

snapped.

"His deal was never with you," Ashe said. "It is, however, binding. Check your email and your accounts, Mrs. Fisher. Your husband signed the paperwork a mere hour before his death. And now that I've convinced a judge the contract is legitimate, the money my employer wired to your account covers the price. Lucille now belongs to Roman Sebastian."

She was a sneaky one, and I had no doubt she'd give the Chameleon a run for her money. As for Corinne, she did as she was told with shaking hands, face reddening as she scanned the screen before looking up in impotent rage. "You can't get away with this."

"It appears you're wrong," Ashe said. "Now, if you don't mind." She gestured at the two of them with the muzzle of her gun. "My employer's property is off limits."

"This is very neat and tidy," I said. "Makes me wonder if that signature is authentic. Or perhaps was forced at gunpoint before his death."

Ashe's dead, dark eyes met mine. "There was no need for such theatrics," she said. "Mr. Fisher approached my employer, not the other way around. The price was more than fair."

"Unless there are priceless diamonds in the car," Corinne snapped, her last-ditch anger spluttering out of her while I sighed.

"Mr. Sebastian has only ever been interested in Lucille," Ashe said. "Not some treasure hunt fairy tale. Now, do I need to call security or will you both leave without further conflict?"

They left, to my surprise, though I didn't miss the longing on Yosef's face, the return to weeping for Corinne as he guided her toward the exit. Which meant it was time for me to go, too, Ashe already slipping away, vanishing out the back door I'd used to enter myself.

While my mind turned and my focus wasn't on the here and now, always a terrible idea. Especially when one was sneaking around places unwelcome. Which was why, as I stepped out into the back hallway, I failed to notice the LAPD officer who, for his part, had no trouble noticing me.

Handcuffs again? Awesome.

CHAPTER SEVENTEEN

IT WAS THEIR COLLECTIVE disappointment that hurt the most. And their quiet. Thing was, I knew I'd done wrong, so it wasn't like they had to go all silent treatment on me. I would have much rathered a solid chewing-out than the discouraged and disenchanted way they all handled my third round in the FBI's custody.

The fact Dune paraded me past my hastily woken father and friends didn't help. Like a walk of shame, really, only without the fun part to begin with. I refused the lure into hangdog, keeping my head up and my eyes front, but it was all a ruse and I was sure they knew it.

Simone came in with me, though her flashing anger and soft dissatisfied tsk said everything she didn't as she saw to it I was again cuffed before leaving the room. Without asking them to free me.

Yeah, she was pissed.

Thing was, I hadn't done this on purpose and I now knew how the killer got in, so that should have counted for something. I stewed over the situation long enough that when the door opened and Elle stepped through I instantly spoke up despite knowing I should have kept my mouth shut.

"The cameras at the back entry are broken," I blurted. "And there was no security whatsoever on the way to the convention hall."

She sat on the edge of the desk, the door opening again. I expected Dune or Miller and instead was rewarded with a stone-faced Very Special Sullenly Stoic (not a sparkle in sight) Andrew Walker, FBI. Elle ignored my father's entry, her expression no longer that dull and resentful nothingness I'd first flinched over. Instead, she laughed. Sadly, exasperated, absolutely. That laugh fading to a resolved chuckle before she grinned as her wrap up.

"You are the most contrary, uncontrolled, rebellious…" Elle looked up at Dad as he joined us with his own reluctance going the way her anger had, turning instead to a kind of surrender that had his face soften and a smile of his own grow as if against his will.

"Has she always been like this?" Elle made it sound like it was Dad's fault, the humor in her voice teasing.

He shrugged that casual G-man shrug of his. "Mostly," he said. "I can't believe you have to work with her."

My detective friend sighed heavily and eye rolled, though her smile never left her, gray eyes now sparkling as she met mine again with good humor far too much in evidence. The two of them could just quit it. "You have no idea," Elle said, the false weight resolute in her surrender to my impossible nature.

"Hardy har," I snapped. "You two are here all week, I presume?"

"Hopefully this is our last show," Elle shot back.

Grumble. "I followed your footsteps, you know."

She didn't answer that the way I expected. "Maybe if you'd trusted me to do the job I was here to do," she said, "I could have told you I'd already shared the information about the lax security at the convention hall with Agent Dune and Detective Miller. Instead, you had to prove a point, which is kind of your thing, so I have myself to blame, really." Her turn to rub at her face with her hands, to toss them once she was done, the sound of her palms slapping the thighs of her jeans loud in the small room. "What are we going to do with you, Petal Morgan?"

"I have trust issues," I grumbled. "Come by them honestly."

"You can only lean into your past for so long looking for blame," she said then, softly and with a casual cruelty I hadn't believed her capable of.

"That's not fair," Dad said. Leave it to him to try to defend me when he knew better.

"No, Dad," I said, sitting back as far as the cuffs would allow, the faint clink of the metal bracelets on the table reminding all of us what my deep dive into such activity got me. "She's right. But that's why I'm here. To let go of Mom and everything I thought she did to make me how I am."

Elle leaned in, poking me in the shoulder with one stiff index finger, kind expression gentle even if her words continued to cut. "You're the only one who makes you," she said. "It's time you took responsibility for it, kiddo."

I thought I *was*. Sullen rejection and that same rebellion she mentioned was beneath me, but I was tired, damn it, and in no state of mind to accept what she had to say.

Yet. Give me a hot minute, yeah?

As for Agent Dune, she looked really happy she'd been dragged out of bed to deal with me again, though Detective Miller was about as rumpled as before, so I could only assume he did sleep in his suit. The FBI agent came immediately to me and uncuffed me herself, not looking at Dad or Elle or even me for that matter.

"You need to look into Corinne Fisher," I said, knowing keeping my mouth shut was the very best option and unable to comply. "Roman Sebastian just paid her a lot of money for Lucille thanks to a contract he claims Edison Fisher signed before his death." Dune didn't respond, backing off. "They were getting divorced," I went on, the running of my mouth unstoppable at this point. "She was having an affair with one of the other buyers, Yosef Moshe."

"Ms. Morgan." Celia Dune's words clipped so

crisply they felt like gunshots. I finally shut up and quit blurting while she fixed me at last with her narrowed eyes, lips a thin line. "You are to leave LA on the next available flight and if I ever see you in my city again, I will personally find a reason to lock you up for the rest of your natural life if I have to fabricate evidence to do it."

Dad's return to grimness preceded his response. "I didn't hear you just say that, Celia." He offered me his hand which I took, stood next to him as he went on. "Threatening an innocent woman who has suffered enough under the circumstances you've forced her into is just another sign to me your time with the Bureau should probably come to an end." Yikes, Dad, what? "The fact you intended to use this case to climb the ladder isn't lost on any of us, Celia, nor is the truth you've failed to advance through promotion or otherwise." Wow, that "or otherwise" was just a little insulting. Then again, if she'd worked with him all those years ago and he'd made SSA (Supervisory Special Agent teaching fresh greenies at Quantico, no less) while she remained a field agent, that did say a lot about how she got the job done— or didn't. "I've already spoken with your supervisor. She's agreed an assessment of your value to the Bureau is long overdue. Now, if you'll excuse us, I'm taking my daughter out of your custody for the last time and if you ever decide to threaten her again, know that I will hear of it. And act on it."

For the third and final time I exited interrogation a free woman. Why then did I feel so very guilty?

CHAPTER EIGHTEEN

THE INEVITABLE FIGHT HAPPENED after we arrived back at the hotel, so at least they gave me that much time to huddle in misery and expectation in the passenger's seat of the SUV while no one said a word to me all the way back to our accommodations.

Of course when they all piled into the suite I shared with Reggie I was firmly convinced the time of reckoning had, indeed, come and they didn't disappoint.

"I have never—"

"Most irresponsible—"

"—were you thinking?"

"—want to get arrested again?"

"Have you completely lost what's left of your fool mind?" In case you hadn't guessed, that was Reggie. She firmly outshouted both Simone and Elle (whose amusement, it turned out, only lasted as long as we were in the FBI offices so had to have been an affectation), though Dad's continuing silence and quiet, if looming, presence shouted about as loudly as his voice was capable of.

"You think I wanted any of this to happen?" I had no intention of engaging with my best friend. She loved me. She'd come all the way to California to support me. I'd dragged her into enough police stations and FBI offices for someone of her background to last a lifetime and she wasn't even in personal trouble. But that recklessness I'd been experiencing since I arrived here wasn't about to cut me slack just yet. Closure? Yeah, more like slashed open wide and gushing. "You think I wanted to come here and find a dead body in my mother's old car instead of getting the goodbye I was looking for?" They all shut up, but I didn't have much time, so I barreled on, full tilt and as hurtful as it was personally agonizing. "You think I go looking for trouble?"

"Don't you?" That was Reggie again, hip cocked, hands in fists at her sides, eyes slits. "Petal, I love you to death but from the moment we met, you've done just that."

I blinked at her, frowning. Remembered, whoopsie daisy, right. The first morning I'd attended Martingale High School I'd chosen to face down the class bully in the basketball court with a firm kick to his very tender parts when he wouldn't leave me alone. Which meant I was suspended after two hours.

For a week.

"That's not fair," I said.

"It never is with you," she shot back. "Making bad choices isn't your fault. Losing Rafe wasn't your fault." I flinched at that, little guilty glance for Simone only catching shade. "Going in debt, trying and failing at a million jobs wasn't you. It's always been someone else to blame, Petal, always!"

"That's not true!" Elle tried the same tactic on me, but you know what? I'd done everything I could in the last year to take full and complete responsibility for my life, to make financial amends, to throw myself into this job I loved. To help people. For money, sure, but that was capitalism for you. Right?

"That's enough, Regina." Dad stepped in. "All of you. Enough." The voice of reason, my hero. Snarl. "We're all tired and it's been a long day." He glanced at his watch. "Our flight leaves in six hours. Try to get some sleep." Reggie muttered something under her breath before storming into her bedroom and slamming the door. Elle and Simone left together, neither of them looking my way, though I did note the lawyer glanced back at me with hurt on her face before the detective firmly closed the way behind them.

Leaving me to face down Dad, something I hadn't been expecting or looking forward to. But when I waited, arms crossed, for him to leave, he didn't. He lingered, his own expression that grim quiet I knew hid more hurt than he'd ever let me see.

"I understand your need to see this through," he said. "But Petal, this is just reckless. You've put your freedom and yourself in danger over and over again, and you haven't even been here thirty-six hours." Who was counting? Dad. Dad was counting. Great. "I didn't want you to come to California, but I stepped aside because you wanted this. I'm regretting not talking you out of it."

"Like you could have," I said. Jaw jutting? You better believe it. Feet planted? Deep as the earth. Ready for a battle I'd lose even if I won? All in, baby.

Dad hesitated. Did he know we were about to say things to each other we'd never be able to take back and would regret for the rest of our lives? Yes, I was sure he did. Did he leave?

Nope.

I guess we were both guilty of stubbornness and the inability to stop even when it was the best choice possible.

I honestly can't remember what I said to him. I know we yelled at one another about Lucille and the jewelry and Roman Sebastian. I'm positive I shouted something about a face watching Mom die that likely sounded incoherent and the crazed fantasy of a madwoman. He didn't hold back either, something about Pops and Jordan and that crushing disappointment I'd been expecting making heated impressions like blows. All culminating in a knock on the door at four in the morning that had Dad fall silent while I shook and wept and glared.

He answered it, though it wasn't hotel security

telling us to shut up or get out. Instead, Elle entered, grabbed him by the arm, and steered him out into the hallway before closing the door in his face. As she turned to me, not moving any nearer, just facing me down, I choked on further sobbing fury while she finally spoke.

"If you won't let us protect you," she said, "don't drag us down with you." She cleared her throat, sighed. Shook her head. "Petal. He loves you. We all do, you crazy ass psycho. Get your act together before you lose him. Before we all walk away." She left then, before I could tell her to get out.

Beg her to stay.

My phone buzzed. A message from Roman Sebastian. *Heard you had further trouble with the FBI. I'm happy to assist.*

I almost told him where to go but ignored the text in favor of reading another that landed a moment later.

Are you over it yet, little sister? Time's ticking.

I threw the phone across the room. Heard it shatter against the wall. Grabbed my gear, tossing aside my jeans in favor of shorts, my sandals for socks and sneakers. And snatched my keycard, slamming my way out of the room, not even trying to hide my exodus this time.

No one followed, so whatever happened from here on in was as much their fault as mine, right?

No, Petal. Actually.

I paused outside the gym, leaning against the wall and staring through the glass door. So tired now I couldn't even contemplate a run, my body exhausted but my brain hurtling at breakneck speed still.

"Are you all right, Ms. Morgan?" His shadow fell over me, that faint scent of BO and sugar. I looked up, bleary and tired, into Marlon Landon's face. His concern didn't soften the edges of anything, just triggered more regret, more guilt, while I shook my head.

"I'm fine," I lied that familiar lie. "Thanks."

He hesitated before leaning against the wall next to me, not touching me, but close enough he could have if he'd wanted to. "I'm so sorry things are going wrong," he said, voice gentle. "You shouldn't have to relive this all over again. You should be able to come back here and just visit with Lucille and your mother and not have to be persecuted like that." A bit of anger crept in, self-righteous and protective. "I get why you came. You had it so hard. It couldn't have been easy growing up without Annette."

He had no clue, did he? Even still. "I should go," I said, not wanting to be mean to him when he was doing his best to be kind. "Thanks, Marlon."

He didn't try to follow me when I walked away, at least. All the energy I'd used to make it to the gym seemed to have burned away, my feet like two lead weights on the ends of my legs, my arms just as heavy, head pounding all over again. I needed to make amends, to apologize to the people I loved, to get the heck out of Cali and do as Dune said.

Never come back.

A flicker from the bar slowed my steps, had me

stop, stare at the commercial I'd come to hate. Mom driving Lucille, that iconic movie moment now a cheap memory used to sell perfume. For what? Nostalgia? No one understood that the past, the heyday they harkened to, the memory of Annette Morgan was as much a lie as the ones that had them buy the crap she peddled post mortem.

I made it to the elevator. Pressed the button. My body standing there, waiting for it to come while my mind—

Went home.

CHAPTER NINETEEN

I HATE THE PARTIES *she throws, so many people, all of them mean and cruel and ugly despite their pretty clothes and their high-pitched voices trying to sound happy and important. She makes me wear things I hate and then parades me around for a bit before making me go to bed.*

Stupid parties. I'm used to being trapped in my room most of the time anyway, but it's worse when there are people because they are so loud and my room is right over the dance floor and bar so all I hear is them all the time and it makes my head hurt.

I hide in her room at the other end of the house where it's quiet. Especially in her closet because I can pull down all her clothes and burrow in like a little animal, like my pet hamster used to under his shavings before it died. He killed him, I know he did, my father killed him because I loved my hamster and he is horrible and mean to me. When he notices me.

Her clothes smell so nice and I know the maid will be

punished for the mess but I don't care because her maid is mean to me, too. They are all mean to me, all the time. Except when I'm invisible and then they aren't mean, but they still hurt me because they don't see me at all. I have no idea what I did to make everyone wish I wasn't there. He doesn't want me around, says it out loud all the time. And Mom only pretends to want me because it makes him mad. As soon as he leaves, she tells me she wishes I was never born so I know she's just using me to hurt him.

I cry into her clothes, blow my nose on the sleeve of her favorite blouse because it will make her angry. Try to tear the fabric but it's too strong for my little fingers. Instead, I crumple it in my fist and hope the wrinkles never come out. She hates wrinkles. I catch the sparkle of the rim of fake jewels around the rim of the shirt's collar.

Remember sneaking into her suite a few days before, the tall man with the dark skin and the white turban over his white suit holding out the black velvet box to Mom, watching with a smile that made his polished black mustache ripple as she opened it. Lots of diamonds in there, a necklace and other things, and a little crown that would make her look like a princess. I wanted to look like a princess, but she'd never let me wear it. Instead, I had to pretend I wasn't there and watch her try it on and wish someone would look at me the way he looked at her.

I hear her storm her way into the room, hear her shouting at someone. The way she'd shouted earlier when she went looking for those diamonds only to find them missing. Accused her maid of theft, hit the girl, even. She'd never hit me, at least. Tonight was different, though, her temper tantrum feels... different. So I peek out into the bedroom to see he's with her.

My father.

She's yelling at him, something about hating him. And he yells back. I hear the word cheating and a few other terrible things he calls her I don't know the meaning of but don't need to because I hear what he means in his voice.

Before he hits her. Hard, across the face. She stares at him, blood trickling from the corner of her mouth. Just before he hits her again.

I close the door, hiding my face in her clothes, mouth open so I don't make a sound when I breathe, but I'm not crying. I don't know why I'm not crying, maybe because I'm so afraid. I hear her screaming, and not angry now. Scared, so afraid. Begging him to stop, blow after blow a thudding strike of fury as he pants and grunts and hits her. I look one more time, but only because she's gone silent, to find she's fallen on the bed and he's crouching over her, hitting her again and again in the face with his fist.

I can't look away, I stare and shake and breathe through my mouth. Until movement makes me blink. Turn my head.

To the partially open door and the face, the pale, male face on the other side, watching as I watch. Not seeing me. Only seeing them.

I close the door one more time and burrow deep to the sound of a very loud bang—

Ding.

I jerked back to the present. Stared into the open elevator so long the doors started to shut again before I realized where I really was, that I was safe, not trapped in Mom's closet under her clothes, the echoing sound of the man I'd thought was my father shooting himself in the head still there in the back of my mind.

And always would be, I realized.

I'd never escape my past. Nor, I accepted then as I stepped onto the elevator and let the doors close behind me, did I want to. What I went through? Was an important part of me. Not something to be discarded or forgotten or erased. I needed to find a way to reconcile the experience, to absorb it, to let it make me stronger, not tear me down the way it did now because I hadn't dealt with it. I could use it, instead of letting it use me.

My mother died and I was there, a silent witness. Her husband killed her. There was nothing I could do to save her.

Nothing anyone—

Not true, Petal Morgan. Someone could have. The man behind the face. A face I knew, didn't I? I recognized, that made me sick thinking about it. A man whose kindness and quest to get to know me and get close to me now felt like a slick of filth on my psyche as much as my skin, a man who wanted me to trust him, to believe him, that he cared about me. A liar as much as any of them. One of them.

I knew who killed Edison Fisher, who pretended to be me to do it.

I just didn't know why.

The elevator started moving, the jerking motion of it rising reminding me I hadn't chosen my floor. I jabbed at the button, but I was too late, already past where I wanted to go. All good. I had thinking to do. A number to call. A killer to turn in to the police.

Except, distraction was again my downfall. The elevator's ding and parting doors caught me off guard, but when I looked up and he entered, looming over me, I knew I was too slow, too late.

As Marlon Landon closed the distance between us with a sad and desperate smile.

"I just wanted you to love me," he whispered.

I moved, but I was slow, so slow, putting myself into his range of motion, into his arms. His right hand rose, cloth in his grip clamping over my mouth, smothering me, the suffocating scent of chemicals making my eyes water, a panicked breath in filling my lungs with the drug.

Darkness descending far too fast, my exhaustion and the lack of oxygen and my endlessly terrible choices contributing to my downfall.

"There's no camera here," he said, touching my hair while the black closed in. "I took care of everything, Annette. You can rest now."

I wasn't my mother, but I didn't get to say so.

My fault. The dark won.

See you soon, Mom.

CHAPTER TWENTY

COOL AIR WOKE ME, the rumble of the engine, the vibration of the car beneath me. I had no idea how long I'd been out, only that as I opened my eyes with groggy confusion, my head turned to the right, the view a mass of lights as LA spread out beneath us. My vision blurred, corrected, blurred again, taking far too long to adjust while I blinked at the city, unable to muster surprise or interest.

A breeze ruffled my hair, my head flopping to the left, to the driver behind the wheel of the racing convertible, his hands grasping the red leather wheel where hers used to, his big, bulky form taking up much more of the seat than her slim delicateness ever managed. No more memories flashed in my mind, at least. The time for living in the past was over.

For as long as I had left to live, I guess it was

meant to be in the here and now.

Lucky me.

Marlon glanced my way, obviously noticing I was awake. I couldn't muster anger or fear, still disoriented from whatever he'd used to subdue me and knock me out, my gaze drifting without real interest over the guardrail on the other side of the winding road and out over the flashing driveways of expensive homes climbing the hills, more light, but all a blur, moonlight pouring over the scenery rapidly flashing past.

"I loved you so much." Marlon's voice was thick with emotion, moisture on his closest cheek evidence he'd been crying. His hands flexed on the steering wheel, big body shifting slightly on the leather seat. "You didn't see me at all, Annette, but I loved you."

"Not my mother." I managed those three words, mouth cotton ball dry, licking my lips, coughing a little. The further I emerged from the drug, the more emotion returned, fear first, but anger a close second. "I'm not my mother, Marlon." He blinked at me, staring so long I had to prod him to look away. "The road."

Marlon jerked back to focusing on driving, swerving to avoid hitting the guardrail on the passenger's side, my heartbeat finally catching up with the situation. An oncoming car laid on the horn, but he ignored the protest and drove on. "I did everything I could to make you notice me," he said, weeping openly. "I made sure you had the best of the best, ran your errands. I did everything you asked of me, Annette. But you didn't *see* me." One hand slapped the wheel in abrupt rage, the car swerving again. I couldn't see the speedometer, but I was sure we had to be doing at least seventy, a perilous speed on this road, a road I knew well.

"You were so young," I said. "Her PA, right? Marlon, Mom didn't have even a second for anyone who wasn't at least her equal. You have to know that." He shook his head, denial and petulance on his face in the low light from the dash, the moonlight pouring over the night sky. It had to be near dawn, right? Unless I'd been out all day. I shuddered at that possibility. No, I was sure it had only been a short time, last of the wee hour darkness soon to be swallowed by sunrise. Which meant I hadn't been out long. Where was he taking me? "Marlon, Mom was selfish and narcissistic and a horrible person. She wasn't worthy of you."

"Stop talking about her like that!" At least he wasn't calling me Annette anymore, though I wasn't sure that was a good thing considering his state of mind. He calmed quickly, though, reaching over with one hand to pat my knee. I batted at his hand, my body not yet willing to respond fully, muscles weak and my whole body trembling from the aftereffects of what he'd done to me. But no way was I letting him get away with putting his hands on me without a fight.

He didn't seem to notice, fingers returning to the wheel as he forced a smile, snuffling and wiping his cheeks on the shoulders of his T-shirt, first right, then left. "You're the love of my life, Annette," he said. "Always were, always will be. I knew when I saw them using that clip from Lucille you'd be back to California. I knew you'd come home someday, and you did. I'm so glad, Annette. Now we can be together and be happy." This dude had fallen so far off his rocker I knew better than to argue. And, I suppose there were worse people to impersonate than my mother, though I really had to think hard to come up with someone. "Now that I have Lucille and you, I have everything. Exactly how I always wanted." He glanced at me again, smiling wider, shyly. "You look so beautiful tonight, Annette. I've always loved that dress on you."

Wait, what? I looked down, realized I no longer wore my T-shirt and shorts, sneakers long gone. Instead, with horror dawning for so many reasons I could barely breathe, I realized I was wearing my mother's dress.

The dress she wore the night she died.

Oh.

My.

GOD.

It was all I could do to keep from screaming, from tearing at the sparkling black fabric, from stripping to my underwear right then and there. Except the second reason for my revulsion hit me, the fact he'd already touched me, that he'd been the one to dress me.

I gagged, choked on the reaction, shuddering while he jerked himself, sudden anxiety on his face making our drive erratic until he caught the swerve.

"It's all right," he said. "I had it cleaned and mended after I bought it. They shouldn't have left it the way they did. It needed to be fixed, made beautiful again." He smiled at me, tremulous and still worried. "Just like you."

There was that much, at least, though did he know? Did he understand it didn't matter if it had been cleaned or not? I still saw the blood on the dress, the way she lay on the bed, still and quiet in death. Her husband's weight on top of her. This dress, this hateful, horrible piece of history, might have been light and flimsy and cut to the daring plunge my mother loved, but it weighed a million pounds in that moment.

I was crying all of a sudden, helplessness and hopelessness and terror all crushing me down into the red leather seat, silent sobs struggling for hysterical control.

This wasn't happening.

A daring and terrible plan seized me, the urge to leap from the car or tackle him or take some violent action squashed just as quickly as it rose, my self-preservation stronger than my panic. He hadn't tied me up, but what was I going to do at 70MPH hurtling down the highway? Despite everything, despite my despair and fear and need to act, I didn't have a death wish.

"I've slept with that dress every night," he said, sinking further into his delusion, my stomach churning in revulsion as he went on, hands scrabbling to brush at the fabric over and over despite knowing it wouldn't help, didn't matter. I had no control over the convulsive action. "I hoped I'd get to see you wear it someday. And here you are." His frown hit in an instant, shadows falling over his face as we turned out of the moonlight and headed deeper into the hills. "I thought you'd like it, Annette. Why don't you like it?"

I made a choice in that moment, to survive. And, in doing so, called up every scrap and shred of her I could, wrapping my mother's memory around me like a cloak before smiling back at him with heavy-lidded eyes, sitting up a little straighter, coyness her favorite when she wanted something.

"Why, it's lovely, Marlon." I reached out and slapped his leg with a soft swipe of my fingertips. "How adorably charming of you, putting little me on such a pedestal." I could hear her voice in my head, see her taking me over and, for the first time in my life, was grateful for my mother. "You do know I'm completely a *mess*." I patted at my hair, realizing then he'd even swept it up, bobby pins poking my fingers.

"You're beautiful," he said, beaming a smile now. "So beautiful, Annette."

"You sweet thing," Mom (I) said, winking. "But a girl needs a moment to herself to be sure she's at her best." I knew this area, now understood where he was taking me and that it was the last place I wanted to go with him. No choice. No options. Unless I could convince him to stop.

All I needed was one shot and this would be all

over.

"Can you say the line?" He wriggled in his seat like a puppy, eager and excited. "Annette, say the line, you know the one."

I did. He didn't have to go into detail. It was the same line being used in the commercials, the most famous line my mother ever spoke from right there in the driver's seat he occupied. "But, sweetheart, darling pet, I can't say it unless the scene is properly set."

He stilled, nodded, sweating now, quick glances in my direction every few seconds making me dizzy. "Please, Annette. Just say it."

Okay, so he wasn't stupid, just nuts. Got it. I drew a breath, knowing keeping him happy for the duration until I had control of myself and the situation my very best option.

"Life is meant to be lived, Lucille!" Yeah, I know. It was a dumb line, and one I hated thanks to the fact she'd loved this ridiculous car more than she ever loved me. But if it meant I bought time and safety I'd repeat it over and over again.

Marlon squealed, his excitement again making his driving erratic. Please, let a cop pull us over. Where were the LAPD when I needed them? They were happy enough to arrest me for a murder I didn't commit, but do you think they were actually there for me when the real killer decided to snap?

Useless, including Celia Dune. She'd be hearing from me about my dissatisfaction with her obvious absence. If I survived.

Instead of rescue, naturally, we hurtled on into the early morning darkness toward the scene of the crime while he danced in his seat.

"Say it again!"

"Life is meant to be *lived*, Lucille." That was pure Mom and had Marlon so worked up I worried I'd gone too far. "Now, you focus on the road, young man." He settled instantly. "I've got a lot more living of my own to do, so you better take good care of me and Lucille."

"Yes, Annette, of course." He wiped at sweat beading on his forehead and upper lip, still grinning. "I can't believe this is really happening."

Tell me about it. "How about that moment for a refresher?" A small gas station squatted on the right. If I could convince him to stop...

"We're almost home," he said, voice dropping to a humming threat. "You can clean up then." His hands tightened on the wheel, knuckles whitening. "You'll be late for your party and we can't have that. Everyone's waiting for you."

I tried pouting. I tried ordering. I even pulled out seduction, as gross as it made me feel. But those last ten minutes before we turned into the driveway I dreaded, Marlon Landon somehow found a well of courage and command sufficient to keep going.

I sank back into the seat as he pulled up to the edge of the construction site, switching off the car and removing the keys before turning to me. I had to be ready, though when I reached for the door handle, I realized how weak I still was. I could barely tighten my hand into a fist. The drug lingered, which meant I was in a lot of trouble.

Worse when he pulled out a gun, my favorite, pointing it at me.

"Time to get the party started, Annette," Marlon said.

CHAPTER TWENTY-ONE

H E CLIMBED OUT, MUZZLE aimed at me the whole time, crossing the front of Lucille before reaching the passenger's door. I had every intention of fighting him, reflexive need to escape ending in me batting ineffectually at him when he unhooked my seatbelt and grabbed my upper arm, jerking me out of the car. The memory of Annette had to be at war with the reality of Petal in his mind, because there was no way he'd have manhandled Mom.

Then again, maybe it was part of his fantasy, loving and abusing my mother. There was a happy thought to keep me warm at night.

If I had another night.

The construction site was empty, the gate opening when Marlon used a key he must have stolen at some point. It made sense, since he obsessed over

Mom, that he did the same about the house.

"You must hate him for changing it," I said, going for distraction if I couldn't manage physical resistance just yet.

"He has no *right*." Marlon's anger had returned, eyes slitted and jaw set, whole body shivering with visible rage. "This is *our* house, Annette. Roman has no right to touch it. But now that we're home, everything will go back to the way it was."

I stumbled in Mom's kitten heels over the wooden boards the construction workers used as a bridge over the muddy ground, Marlon forcing me forward, the tight and sweaty grip he used making me cringe from his touch. He pushed the front door open, a different key this time letting us inside. "You've worked on the site," I said, understanding dawning.

The dirt on his steel-toed boots wasn't from carelessness. I'd thought it an odd choice. Instead, it was a necessity. And the reason the keys in his possession gave him access to the site.

"I was here yesterday," he said. "I came back to work after the cops let me go. Saw you here." Of course he was. "I saw Roman talking to you. He never loved you, Annette. He just wanted to possess you, like everyone else."

"Even you, Marlon?" I finally resisted, pulling free. He let me, staring down at me in the dimness of the interior of the house while I hugged myself and shook, knees weak, thighs trembling from the aftereffects of the drug. And fear. Yup, that, too.

"You want to possess her, isn't that right?"

He didn't respond with words, gesturing for me to keep going. To the staircase, untouched as of yet, the same white marble and wrought iron railing from my childhood making me flinch. I climbed slowly, clicking of Mom's shoes on the stone treads like a knell of a bell foretelling my end but I had no choice.

No choice at all.

He didn't have to tell me where he wanted me to go, though I did consider pretending to want to go to the party. That at least would distract him a little longer. But his focus was on the second floor, the west wing and the final destination I was positive would be the place I died.

Like she did.

Where she did.

I sobbed, allowing myself to weep, to let out the fear and aching sorrow, grief and terror intermingling, the little girl I was following along with me as we walked the long hall to the door at the end, through it and into Mom's suite.

It had been emptied, bed gone, walls stripped to the studs, floor still hardwood but buffed down to rough grain instead of the shining surface I remembered, white oak my mother's favorite. The absence of furniture, of anything personal, made it easier to stand there, to gain control of my tears and my emotions, to wipe at my nose and face and inhale before turning to face him from where I stood in the middle of the empty room.

Empty to the naked eye but packed solid with

memories so hurtful I ached from them.

"You were here." I hadn't intended to antagonize him. It was the worst possible choice. But now that I was here and my weeping run its course? Oh, the rage. The utter and complete fury at this entire circumstance. His gun and his crazy and his needs be damned. "You watched her die, Marlon."

He flinched from me, gun wavering, looming in the dark room, no longer threatening to me. He could kill me if he wanted. I dropped my arms from around myself, contempt rising with my rage, my mouth twisting with it while he shook his head.

"I wouldn't—"

"You," I jabbed a finger at him, voice rising, "you let her die that night, Marlon." I threw my anger at him, more a weapon than the bullets he threatened me with, each word striking him in physical reaction while he blubbered and shook his head in endless denial. "You watched from the door." I pointed at it, too. "You saw him, what he did to her and you stood there and *watched*."

"I wanted to save her!" His wail was half shout, half scream of hurt. "I wanted to make him stop."

"Why didn't you?" I let him see just how much I despised him, hoped it cut him deep. Succeeded from the way he dropped his gaze, refused to look at me, head turning from side to side now, not in denial but in a desperate need to keep from seeing. I closed the distance between us, challenging him (stupid, Petal, stupid), not caring what might happen next because he'd stood there and watched (so did you, kid) and did nothing, (just like you, little girl) and let her die (pots and kettles, Petal Morgan). "Why didn't you help her?"

I wasn't talking to him anymore. Obvs.

Why didn't I help my mother?

You better believe I'd flinched from that question my entire life. Excuses like, *I was just a little girl*, and, *he would have killed me, too*, doing nothing to rub out the truth of the matter. That I'd peeked. I'd heard her screaming and him hitting her and I'd seen what he'd done, right? I'd looked and I knew, knew, she was dying. And I hid. In her closet. In her stuff, in her scent. And let him.

Because I hated her.

I sobbed all over again, doubling over, clutching at my throat that threatened to close over from the ball of burning emotion choking me, the blame and shame and guilt a suffocating and sweltering wave of flaming accusation I'd lived with my entire life.

I let my mother die because I was a bad person.

Except.

In that horrible, hurtful moment as I screamed out my pain, the agony and grief cracked. Broke, as I feared I was broken. And fell away at last, finally, in a shower of sparks that had me seeing stars as I fought for air.

There was nothing I could have done to save her.

He would have killed me if he'd caught me there.

I didn't kill my mother.

I didn't let her die because I hated her.

My mother died because of her.

It wasn't my fault.

It wasn't.

Deep breath, Petal. Deep breath.

Marlon stared at me, gun hand wavering, mouth hanging open, his own face wet with fresh tears. I sniffled, two-handed the moisture from my face, heart and soul settling, emotions drained dry. When I stared up at him, his hesitant and terrified expression more deer in the headlights than threatening, I nodded.

"Coward," I said.

He shuddered. "I was afraid." Marlon choked himself. "I loved her, and I couldn't save her." The gun dropped further, his gaze now distant. "I tried to save her. After he shot himself. I tried, but it was too late."

What?

"She was still alive?" I had no idea. "She. You." Rage returned and I lunged for him, pounding on him with both fists, a sudden spike of adrenaline using the remnants of my strength. My attack didn't last, falling to my knees in her dress on the floor, fury all that was left of me.

Marlon stared down at me, gun now hanging at his side, infinite sorrow on his face. "I tried to save her," he whispered. "She begged me to. Promised me everything. But I couldn't move. I stood there and watched her die."

"Why?" My turn to wail.

"She rejected me that night." He wavered, shrugging, swaying like a tree about to fall. "In that dress. At the party. I found the courage to tell her I loved her, and she was cruel." His face twisted, mouth trembling, whole body shaking violently, fist closing around the gun again, though he used it to gesture instead of shoot. "She mocked me and walked away from me and was going to get me fired." He shuddered all over, a dog shedding water. "I just wanted to talk to her." His voice cracked but settled, his own emotions drained, body sagging forward, gun against his thigh. "I needed to convince her. I came up here, followed her. Watched him beat her. Wanted to beat her too." Menacing, now, violence behind his eyes. "When it was over and he was dead, I came to see her. And she begged me to save her. But she lied, she lied about everything. I knew if I saved her she'd just hurt me again. So, I just watched."

"That makes you a murderer," I said.

He nodded. Sighed. "I know," he said. "That's what made it easier to kill Edison Fisher."

CHAPTER TWENTY-TWO

I HADN'T EXPECTED HIM to just confess like that, though I shouldn't have been surprised after everything we'd just gone through. Still, the shift in topic of conversation had me stunned and gaping, something Marlon didn't seem to notice.

"He never valued Lucille, Annette." He was back to thinking I was Mom, apparently, good for him. I forced myself to my feet, unsteady but refusing to remain on my knees, while Marlon carried on, making no move to help. "None of them did. Not that Yosef or Ashe. She's just working for Roman anyway, and I couldn't let Roman have Lucille."

"You found out Edison was selling to him," I said. "How?"

"I overheard him talking on the phone," Marlon said. "When I was working outside. I knew he'd cheated, that he was going to get Lucille and she'd be locked away and I'd never get another chance ever." No crying this time, just jaw-jutting defiance. "It was really easy to pretend to be you." He blinked. "Your daughter, Petal." Back and forth and around we go with the crazy dance. "I read about you. *Her.*" Marlon ran his free hand over his face, surfacing from delusion briefly. "I knew about your agency, about who you became." How nice for him. "I finally found you thanks to that case you did, the one in the psychic house." I had Valentina June to thank for the publicity, though it hadn't been much. That kind of recognition meant I needed to start wearing wigs for sure. "I bought a burner, used it to text Edison. Had him convinced the jewels were in Lucille but I was the only one who knew how to find them." He smiled briefly, a startled and hopeful look that faded almost immediately. "I never imagined you'd show up at the auction personally."

Whatever, jerkface. "Why did you kill him?"

Marlon hesitated, shaking his head. "I never meant to," he said. "I just wanted to talk him out of selling to Roman. When he found out it was me and not you, he laughed at me. Sat in Lucille's front seat and laughed at me." His jaw clenched again, face flattening into anger. "I grabbed his lanyard to drag him out but he fought me, so I choked him with it." He met my eyes with his own full of that same horrible hope. "I left him as a tribute to you, Annette," he said, sliding back into his internal monologue with the dead woman he'd watched breathe her last. "I knew you'd appreciate the sentiment." Funny, Mom probably would have. Said a lot for her, huh? "Did you, Annette?" He wavered toward me, gun rising a little. "Did you enjoy my gift?"

This had to end, and there was only one way as far as I was concerned. I needed that gun and if it meant putting a bullet in a mentally ill man, you bet your booties I'd be pulling the trigger. Trouble was, taking it from him wasn't going to be easy in my condition. The way he stared at me now, how his own rage found a focus, blame rising, it was easy to guess his internal cogs were now shifting toward hate.

For Mom.

For me.

In the end, it was easier than I thought. I doubt Marlon even suspected I'd fight back, likely because Mom wouldn't have. He was so lost in his delusion when I stepped forward and kicked him in the side of his right knee, he buckled instantly, eyes widening, mouth a gaping black O of surprise, while I hit him as hard as I could across the bridge of his nose with my forearm even as I reached for the gun and jerked it out of his unresisting hand.

Stood over him while he sobbed, hands cupping his bleeding septum, shaking at my feet. Was it wrong my finger slid over the trigger? That I thought about it? Actually saw myself squeeze, felt the buck of the gun? Watched the bullet tear a nice, neat hole through his forehead?

"Petal." He had to interfere, didn't he? Dad

appeared at the door, his own gun out, Elle panting behind him. I had been so lost in my own fantasy, I hadn't heard them running toward me, which they'd clearly done, both out of breath, both now circling to flank the sobbing Marlon where he knelt at my feet. "Please, Pet, put the gun down. It's okay, kiddo."

I looked up, met his eyes. "This piece of crap watched Mom die," I said. "She was still alive, Dad. After he shot himself. She lived. He could have saved her."

Dad stopped, didn't say anything for a long moment. "Petal," his voice cracked, such a rarity for the stoically stubborn and rigid Andrew Walker. "Honey, I'm so sorry. For all of it. But you have to put the gun down, now, okay?"

I shook my head. "I lived my whole life thinking I was to blame, Dad," I said. "But I really was just a little girl. He would have killed me too if I'd tried to save her. But *him*." I jabbed the gun in Marlon's direction. "He watched her *die*." It seemed so important Dad understand that.

"Ms. Morgan." I didn't know Agent Dune had come along, or Detective Miller, blinked at the sight of the two also entering the room, guns drawn. "Marlon Landon will go to prison for what he's done, I promise you that. But if you don't put that gun down right now…" she inhaled slowly. "Please don't make me shoot you."

"Let me handle this, Celia," Dad snapped. "No one is shooting anyone. Pet." Dad put his gun away under his jacket, slowly, hands extended while I started to shake and cry again because he was here, wasn't he? For me, like he had been that night. Like—

I spun on Dune, careful to keep the gun out of play. "I remember you now," I said.

She flinched. Actually flinched. For good reason. "Ms. Morgan—"

—"*She probably had it coming.*" *I peek out the tiny gap I allow in the door at the sound of a woman's voice, hoping for someone to save me. She's tall, in a suit, with a lovely face. But she's harsh and cruel, I hear it in her tone of voice, in the rigid cynicism in her expression.*

"It's called compassion, Celia," his voice interrupts her. "Find some."

"Yes, sir," she says, glancing away, toward me while not seeing me, lips twisting in disdain. "I'm just saying. She had a reputation. Everyone knows it."

"Let's focus on the facts, please," he says.

"It's not hard to see what happened." She turns her back to me, gesturing though I can't see what she's pointing at. "They fought, he beat her to death then shot himself." She makes a soft grunting sound. "Messy but pretty cut and dried." She sounds so happy about that. "You do know this case is going to make our careers."

"Your career is the last thing I care about right now," he says.

"Sir," someone calls out. "The daughter is missing."

The woman sighs like that's a huge bother. "Just what we need, a minor to deal with."

Her statement hurts. She's just like all the others, like Mom and her so-called friends. It's true no one wants me so

I'm going to stay here in the closet forever. Except I jerk back, closing the door more firmly than I planned. Realize my mistake at the sound of footsteps closing in on the door. I burrow back into the pile of clothes, shaking, trying not to cry, when he opens it. Looms over me, a shadowy figure backlit and terrifying.

Until he crouches and the light softens his edges, big hands reaching out toward me. "Hello, sweetheart," he says, that same deep voice now soft and full of kindness. "I'm Andy. What's your name?"

"Is that the kid?" The woman stands behind him. She's frowning, judging. "Don't bother yourself with her, sir. I'll get a uniform."

"I'll take care of it." He's harsh with her finally, though when his blue eyes meet mine, I see kindness. And, in a world where trust is at a premium, in a lifetime taught that giving that trust to others will mean cruelty and betrayal, I can't help it.

He's different.

And then I'm scurrying out of the dark and the clothes and I'm wrapping my arms around his neck, burying my face in his shoulder. "Petal," I whisper.

"Hello, Petal," he says. "Everything's going to be okay now."—

"I remember you," I whispered again, Dune's flinch turning to sullen acceptance as I came back from the past. "Guess Mom's death didn't make your career after all. Sorry mine won't help you, either."

Whatever her reaction to the truth, her truth, I couldn't care less. I had someone more important to deal with. Looked up at the man I adored so much, who saved me once, saved me so many times, he had no idea. And offered the gun to my dad, my hero.

He took it, handing it off to Elle as he tugged me out of Marlon's reach, letting the others cover the still weeping and now fully broken man while my dad held me.

Like he did that night.

And I cried all over again.

CHAPTER TWENTY-THREE

I SWUNG MY FEET, now bare, Mom's kitten heels tossed aside, my butt planted on the bumper of the ambulance, a gray blanket around me as the EMT finished her quick exam. I wished I had clothing to replace the dress I still cringed from, regardless of its present state of cleanliness compared to the last time Mom wore it.

Some things just couldn't be washed clean no matter how much effort you made.

"I'm fine," I said, realizing the EMT was waiting for some response I'd missed the opening to. "Thank you."

"You're very lucky," she said with a smile and a squeeze to my shoulder. Handed me a bottle of water. "You should have a doctor check you out, but it looks like there's no lasting effects to the drug he gave you."

Dad waited for her to leave, the morning's new sunlight casting a long shadow as he stood in front of it, tall body silhouetted until he crossed its path and joined me. I made room, leaning into him when he slid his arm around my shoulders, resting my head against him while Miller and Dune led the handcuffed Marlon away.

"I'm sorry, Dad," I said.

"Me too, Pet." Dad kissed my forehead but didn't let me go.

"I've spent all these years thinking I let her die, that I didn't act because I hated her." I sighed, toying with the cap of my untouched water, twisting it on and off again, crackle of the snapping seal louder than I expected. "But I realized that wasn't true. I really did love her, even though she never loved me. Couldn't. Didn't know how." I pushed back my hair, some of it come free from the bobby pins and hanging in my eyes. "I always thought that meant there was something wrong with me. That I was broken. It made it so hard to let you love me." A tear escaped, a small one, my reservoir of weeping almost dried up but able to squeeze that last bit of regret out. "I would have saved her if I could have. And I would have loved you and Pops and Jordan and Rafe so much better if I hadn't…" Stopped talking because I didn't need to say anymore, did I?

He nodded against my hair. "None of this was your fault, Petal." Dad sighed, hugged me with both arms, rocking me a little. "I tried so hard to show you, but I'm not the best at the whole showing how I feel thing, in case you missed it."

I choked out a laugh. "No, you? Really?"

We chuckled together.

"I can't believe I forgot such an important detail," I said.

"The mind is a funny thing," Dad said. "It did its best to protect you."

"Like you always have." I sat back, looked into his blue eyes. "I never said thank you, Dad. Or I love you nearly enough." I hugged him tight, arms around his chest, face pressed to his neck, heart aching but with joy now instead of judgment and guilt. "I'll make it up to you and Pops and Jordan," I said, voice muffled by his shirt collar. "I promise."

He squeezed me tighter. "There's nothing to make up," he said. "Pet, you lived through something no one, let alone a child, should have to. The truth was and remains that your mother's husband murdered her. End of story." I let him go, nodding. "Even if Marlon Landon called for help... kiddo, I saw the coroner's report. She wouldn't have made it to the hospital. He couldn't have saved her, either."

Oddly, that was comforting to know. "I wanted closure," I said. "And for this to be over once and for all. As usual, my methods are questionable, but I got the job done."

Dad laughed at that. "Oh, Petal." And, to my shock, broke down and cried.

Not for long, mind you. This was Andrew Walker we were talking about. But the vulnerability he showed in that moment healed me more than he would ever know.

The sound of a car pulling up had us both sniffling and wiping our eyes, black car rolling into the scene like a movie, stirring a cloud of yellow dust in the early morning sunlight. The sight of Ashe Yoshida exiting the limousine closely followed by Roman Sebastian making me stiffen, protective need to shield Dad from my sperm donor triggering belligerence.

Ashe kept her distance, but Roman joined us, if staying a few feet away, tall body in a carefully tailored cream linen suit, brown shoes dusty from the walk. "I came as soon as I heard," he said. Met Dad's eyes. "Agent Walker, I want to thank you for taking such good care of Petal all these years."

He made it sound like there was a pending shift in ownership and he could just shove that attitude somewhere uncomfortable and maybe fatal.

Instead of overreacting like I clearly was, Dad offered his hand. "Mr. Sebastian," he said in his best Super Sparkly Special Agent voice.

"I'd like a moment with my daughter," Roman said.

I inhaled to tell him to shove off. While Dad glanced at me, expression mild, faint smile on his lips.

"Only if it's okay with *my* daughter," he said.

I had never loved Dad so much as I did in that moment and almost laughed out loud. Almost. Because I was still pissed, so angry, I managed instead just a snort. It was enough.

Dad kissed my cheek, one big hand tucked into my hair, holding me to him like he had when I was little before letting me go. Not symbolic or anything because I wasn't going anywhere.

He was stuck with me now for reals.

As for Roman, he held still and quiet until Dad nodded pleasantly and walked off, joining Elle near the SUV, the two waiting for me without appearing to wait for me because they were professionals, yo. Roman's visible distress softened me just a bit, enough I held off on the scathing *get lost* speech I'd been working on since he arrived and listened.

"I have something for you." He held out his hand, palm down, fingers fisted around the contents. I reached out, a little reluctant, only to have him drop a small metal object into my grasp.

I stared at the key, shrugged. Tossed it back. "I have one of my own," I said.

Roman had caught it deftly, stepped forward and set it on the bumper next to me. "You misunderstand," he said, glancing over his shoulder where Marlon had parked Mom's car. "I'm not giving you the key, Petal." He paused a long moment while I absorbed what he meant, suddenly unable to breathe. "I bought her for you."

He left then, getting in his limo, Ashe going with him, leaving me to retrieve the key. To stand and walk across the construction zone to the gate. Through it. To her. To Lucille.

Mom's favorite possession now belonged to me.

She'd have hated that.

CHAPTER TWENTY-FOUR

W HY MY EX-HUSBAND THOUGHT it was appropriate to continually text-message me with demands to know I was okay when his girlfriend was with me was beyond me. Never mind he'd recently taken a bullet for me, right? Raphael Van Dorn needed to get his priorities straight.

Just kidding. I had the weirdest life. And the most awesome people to share it with. The funny part? Even after everything I'd gone through, done (and maybe because of it) I wouldn't trade it for anything.

Elle's tight hug and whispered, "You didn't die," when I'd finally joined her and Dad with Lucille's key in my hand. It was all the making up we needed to do. How cool was that?

When we arrived at the ER, Simone and Reggie were waiting for us. My lovely lawyer friend held off for about a second before throwing her arms around me and squeezing me until I choked.

"I don't care how often you get arrested," she gushed. "I'll always defend you." Blushed like that didn't come out right while I laughed.

And that was sufficient for her.

Reggie was a little more complicated, though as she sat next to me in the hospital while the ER doctor checked me over, she softened incrementally as I shared the story of what happened with the people I adored. Waited until Dad, Elle and Simone left to talk to the doc. Then grabbed me the moment we were alone, and sobbed on my shoulder before punching me in the arm so hard I flinched.

"If you ever scare me like that again..."

"No promises," I'd grinned.

She laughed, hugged me one more time. "You're such a jerk."

"Yeah," I'd said. "I know. Thank you for loving me, Reg."

More tears and that was that.

Which left me oddly calm and composed despite the last forty eight hours and the emotional outlay not to mention being drugged, yeah, hadn't forgotten about that. We were late leaving, a whole day late, thanks to that same ER doctor who erred on the side of caution and admitted me to be sure the drug Marlon gave me was out of my system. I'm sure he would have sent me home if it wasn't for Dad looming and suggesting at least four times said doctor do just that.

Dads. Snort.

I checked my phone again while my people pushed aside the last of their giant diner breakfasts, quiet conversation carrying on around me, though the sandwich center I made between Dad and Reggie wasn't lost on me. I hadn't been alone since Dad and Elle arrived on the scene and I figured I had a long wait before they'd allow me any solo time.

I'd take it.

Didn't keep me from the privacy of my thoughts, though or the text message from the Chameleon that arrived shortly after I settled in my hospital bed still there, undeleted, and I read it for what had to be the hundredth time while my loved ones chattered around me.

See you soon, little sister.

Mixed feelings about being the sibling of an international assassin and thief and the daughter of yet another international criminal? Naw. Why do you ask? Groan.

The latest message I deleted without reading. If I thought Rafe texted me frequently, he had nothing on Yosef Moshe. I could only take so many pleas (*I'll give you anything you ask*), demands (*that car was meant to be mine and I'm calling my lawyer about the contract*) and giant offers of money (he topped out at a million, the fool). My initial, *Lucille isn't for sale*, was met with further bullying. The man had no idea who he was dealing with.

I didn't take bullying lightly and nor did I let it influence me even a little. Neither did dragging

Corinne into things, having her call me—turned out this wasn't Edison's first marriage and his will left everything to his living children, how sad for her. I listened to the weeping confession of her dead husband's betrayal for all of about sixty seconds before hanging up. And refusing to answer further calls. She could weep on Yosef's shoulder as far as I was concerned.

Didn't matter. They could blow hot air and threats and money offers all they wanted. For some people it came down to the principle, but I knew for them it was the pipedream of Mom's diamonds, worth far more than a million at this point, I could only imagine.

Besides, when I said no, I meant it. Dug in my heels about it. Stubborn? You betcha. I had Mom to thank for that. For a lot of things, now that I was able to think about her with truth instead of hurt. Put myself in her shoes (just, not her dress again, thanks), and try to see the world from the eyes of a girl famous too young, hurt herself by who knew how many people, raised in a lifestyle that bred narcissism and ego.

I hadn't fully forgiven her yet, but I was working on it. As for the car I'd hated like it was a rival sibling out of the blue?

Lucille had come home to her last owner.

And no, Paxton Hunter, thanks for asking three times. I wasn't interested in auctioning her off, either. Seriously, these people needed to check in with one another before I blocked them.

Whoops. Too late.

"You're sure you're okay to stay?" Dad said that quietly from where he sat next to me, the reason I was remaining in LA despite my initial desire to the contrary busy laughing with Reggie across from me.

"I'm good, Dad," I said. And I was. The thing about facing down trauma, it might have been messy, but it did wonders for my soul. "Besides, Simone needs me." She'd been tentative when she admitted she was staying behind, only telling us she had a request from a client and that she could use my help after we all bugged her about it until she caved.

Because we were awesome like that.

The fact Reggie instantly offered to assist while Elle's droll grin as she tossed her own gloves in the ring had me smiling. And feeling better about myself and my life and the people I'd been lucky enough to wrangle into it than I had in a very long time.

Ever, Petal. Say it like you mean it.

"I'll have her back in a few days, Andy," Simone said, overhearing despite Dad's attempt to keep it quiet.

He smiled at her, kissed my temple. "She's a big girl," he said. "And she gets the job done. Just, please." He winced. "Don't get arrested, okay? And steer clear of Celia Dune."

She'd been reluctant to meet my eyes after I'd recalled her treatment of me, of Mom, at the murder scene. Regret or just guilt she'd been found out? Whatever the case, I hadn't made a friend, but if she thought she could push me into leaving LA when I wanted to stay?

We had the bullying conversation already. Just refer to that and carry on.

"You realize you just jinxed it, Andy." Reggie grinned at me while Dad groaned.

"Then I guess I'd better leave before I make things worse." He slid out of the booth, Reggie and myself both exiting to allow him to stand. I stopped him as he pulled some money out of his wallet.

"On me," I said. "Dad, can I ask a favor?"

He put his money away, nodding. "Anything, Pet." I know he didn't mean to let the emotion out, for his voice to crack. I squeezed his hand and waved to the girls.

"Dad and I have something to do," I said. "I'll meet you at the hotel."

They waved in return, the three deep in conversation as I led my dad out, paying the bill for everyone on my way past the counter, generous tip making the busy waitress smile.

I stepped out into the California sunshine, inhaling deeply of desert air and sun-warmed asphalt on the busy sidewalk, Lucille parked next to the SUV we'd rented. "I have somewhere I need to go," I said. "But I need to go alone. I'm going to need a ride back. Do you mind?" I glanced at my phone. "I know you have a flight but I should have you to the airport in time."

Dad shook his head, frowning a little. "Let's go."

He followed me as I drove, avoiding the insanity of LA's giant highways, taking the side streets with the top down. I got more than a few toots of appreciation for Lucille's shining and sleek appearance, sunglasses hiding most of my face, my hair in a tight pony, feeling more like Mom than I really should have.

Not a bad thing anymore, turned out.

It was a half hour drive to Santa Monica and Palisades Park and I actually enjoyed every minute of it. The anticipation of saying goodbye to my old life used to fill me with dread at having to face what happened. The reality, especially now, felt far different and I actually even turned on the radio, sang along to some songs, let myself and my old pain go on that short but cathartic drive.

I found the lookout bluff I was searching for, the one where Mom had her photo shoot with Lucille. She'd dragged me along, naturally, to admire her. And I had, as much as I'd hated her, too. Wished I was the center of attention. Made a nuisance of myself more than once, to the point she finally drove home without me, making her assistant take care of me.

The day of the party. The day she died. Perfect.

I parked at the edge of the lookout, on the far end of the guardrail where a short section had been damaged, the gap unrepaired, and sat a moment, looking over the water. I heard him park near me, get out, felt him climb into the passenger's seat, all without saying a word. Took in the ocean breeze, my dad beside me, before sighing.

"I remember the day you came for me." We'd

never talked about it, but so many memories had been stirred, come to the surface, I finally wanted to. "It was the sound of your voice, Dad." I smiled at him, chest tight with happiness wanting to come out in tears. "They never told me you were trying to adopt me. Oh, maybe they said something about Agent Walker, but I didn't associate that name with you. To me, you were always Daddy. Did you know that?" His nostrils flared as he shook his head, held eye contact despite the rim of moisture rising in his own gaze. Refusing to look away. "I was playing with the teddy bear you sent me. I remember being sad, feeling alone. And then I heard your voice, and I knew everything was going to be okay." I'd run to him immediately, the tall savior I remembered as the only man I ever trusted, who swung me up into his arms and held me the whole time he wrapped up what he needed to do that day at the foster home before taking me away from that life forever. "And I was right, Dad. Everything has been okay." I reached out, squeezed his hand, laughed a little. "I know I've been a screwup, but the thing is, I had the chance to be. I knew I was safe. And because of you, I have this crazy and unconventional and really awesome life." I exhaled deeply, still smiling, unable to stop. "I've spent far too long trying to figure out how to be who you wanted me to be. But that was my mistake."

"I only ever wanted you to be you and be happy." Dad's voice was thick, but he managed.

"I know that now," I said. "Thanks for putting

up with me while I figured myself out." I did a little dance of happiness right there in my seat. "Dad, I finally did."

His chuckle ended in a kiss to my temple. "You did," he said. "I always knew you would."

I let his hand go to grasp the steering wheel, feeling the leather under my skin, like I could touch Mom by doing so. "This car represents everything I hated about her." I turned to smile at him again while he nodded one more time. "Everything about my old life that I blamed for being broken, for making a mess of my life. But it's not Lucille's fault." I let go of the wheel. "I've been wanting to say goodbye. It's time to do that." I couldn't help the private little smirk that I know had to have twisted my face into wickedness because Dad grinned easily back, surprise on his face, and anticipation. "I'm ready for that *sayonara.* But not before I share the secret even my mother didn't know about."

Dad's eyes widened a little, leaping to a conclusion I knew he would because he was that good of an agent and a dad. "The jewelry? Is the story real?"

Instead of answering with words, I climbed out of the car while he watched in confusion. "I told them over and over again," I said. "Mom didn't hide the diamonds in Lucille." I flipped the front seat back forward, reaching down and pulling loose the flap at the bottom before unzipping the leather cover. It was awkward, I wasn't eight anymore. But my fingers found the hole in the foam, slid around what I was looking for and, one piece after another, I pulled out a necklace, a ring, two dangling earrings, a bracelet and, finally with a grunt of effort, the tiara.

Dropping them one at a time into Dad's open hands.

"Petal." He stared at them, then at me. "You?"

I winked. Leaned against Lucille, crossing my arms over my chest. "I was so furious with her," I said. "She was so exited about the gift. I knew she wanted to wear them that night, so I decided to punish her." It all seemed far off now, surreal, like it happened to someone else. "I snuck into her room and stole the diamonds from the box and hid them here. In the car she loved more than me." I laughed, shaking my head. "She was furious, Dad. I felt so powerful that day. For the first time ever. Even more so when I left *that*." I pointed to the dash under his knees where I'd then carved my name for posterity. "She never knew and that made it more delicious." I reached down, tried on the ring, admired the giant diamond in the sunlight, the heavy platinum setting garish and too big for my finger. A relic of another time and place. "I forgot all about it, you know. The trauma of losing Mom. Until the auction, when the subject of the diamonds came up. And I remembered." The little girl I was, doing triple damage to my mother, destroying the inside of her seat, stealing from her and vandalizing her car all in one short burst of rebellion I never got to repeat or really enjoy. "She died that night, but she's been with me all along. I'm ready for her to go, now." I met his eyes, smiled. "I know it's against the law. But can you turn the other cheek, just this once?"

He was still confused, I could see it in his face. "Whatever you need, Petal."

I motioned for him to get out and he did, hands juggling diamonds while I bent and retrieved a chunk of broken asphalt, weighing it in my hand a moment before half sitting with my foot on the brake. I jammed the chunk of pavement into the clutch, holding it down, then slid the shift into neutral. Stood, one hand on the door, the other on the dash.

And pushed.

It didn't take much to get her rolling. Just a little effort, really, as she eased forward, gathering speed before the edge. I had time to slam the door before she tipped in slow motion, caught on the lip of the cliff, her final teeter sending her over the side and out of sight.

I rushed forward to watch, grinning like I was eight all over again and wasn't this the grandest joke, hands jammed in my back pockets, Dad coming to stand next to me. Lucille tumbled and crashed her way to the rocks below, damage done, and though Hollywood had me hoping she'd burst into flames at the bottom, she merely crumpled like an old tin can between two giant teeth of stone, tearing her almost in half before the waves crashed into her and dragged her down further, water swallowing her as she sank to the bottom.

"'Bye, Lucille," I said.

'Bye, Mom.

Looking for more Petal Morgan? Have no fear, book eight is coming soon! Look for your copy of *The Rock Star Deception* at all fine retailers!

MASQUERADE INC. COZY MYSTERIES: EIGHT

THE Rock Star DECEPTION

PATTI LARSEN

USA Today Bestselling Author

And don't miss USA Today best-seller,
The High Tide Deception, available in ebook!

AUTHOR NOTES

MY VERY DEAR READER:
No shame, I cried through most of this book. Petal's tragic past was hard to write about, though she knew it needed to be done so I trusted her and I'm glad I did.

I had intended to stop at book six, *The Protection Deception*, for now, but she had so much more to say I couldn't bear to leave this book unwritten for the few months it will take to return to her story. That being said, she has two more mysteries already lined up for me, as was foreshadowed with the girls staying in LA for Simone's client. So, keep your eyes open for *The Rock Star Deception* and *The Engagement Deception*, coming this summer.

For now, Petal is satisfied to let me carry on now that her history is resolved and whatever closure she was looking for is achieved.

While I wrap up my seven submissions for **Whiskered Mysteries**, I'm working on a lot of other projects. This year has been very productive so far and I don't see that slowing down. That means you'll be seeing more **Phoebe Monday** with her pending book three, *Drawn To Death* coming shortly as well as a brand-new character I can't wait for you to meet. The **Whitewitch Island Paranormal Cozies** introduce you to retired **Artemis Guild Inquisitor Georgia Drake**, her giant adopted mastiff Benjamin, and two raven companions, Conscio and Caprice. While she might be officially off paranormal cases, she quickly finds moving to a "normal" island and letting slip her past means assisting the local sheriff in a string of murders while dealing with her own past. Look for book one, ***Dead Even***, coming up next!

Thank you for reading and, for now, as always, safe and heathy out there and happy reading.

Best,

Patti

ABOUT THE AUTHOR

EVERYTHING YOU NEED TO know about me is in this one statement: I've wanted to be a writer since I was a little girl, and now I'm doing it. How cool is that, being able to follow your dream and make it reality? I've tried everything from university to college, graduating the second with a journalism diploma (I sucked at telling real stories), am an enthusiastic member of an all-girl improv troupe, Side Hustle (if you've never tried it, I highly recommend making things up as you go along as often as possible) and I get to teach and perform with an amazing group of women I adore. I've even been in a Celtic girl band (some of our stuff is on YouTube!) and was an independent film maker (go check out the Lovely Witches Club at https://www.lovelywitchesclub.com). My life has been one creative thing after another—all leading me here, to writing books for a living.

Now with multiple series in happy publication, I live on beautiful and magical Prince Edward Island (I know you've heard of Anne of Green Gables) with my multitude of pets.

I love-love-love hearing from you! You can reach me (and I promise I'll message back) at patti@pattilarsen.com. And if you're eager for your next dose of Patti Larsen books (usually about one release a month) come join my mailing list! All the best up and coming, giveaways, contests and, of course, my observations on the world (aren't you just dying to know what I think about everything?) all in one place: http://bit.ly/PattiLarsenEmail.

Last—but not least!—I hope you enjoyed what you read! Your happiness is my happiness. And I'd love to hear just what you thought. A review where you found this book would mean the world to me— reviews feed writers more than you will ever know. So, loved it (or not so much), your honest review would make my day. Thank you!